TWILIGHT
ZONE
for
CHRISTIANS

To
ANGELA

MICHAEL EDWIN Q.

TWILIGHT ZONE
for
CHRISTIANS

A COLLECTION OF SHORT STORIES

Library of Congress Catalog Number: 2017951751
1. Fiction
2. Fiction: Christian – Suspense

Editing: Melissa Foster Sanz
Cover Design: Alexander von Ness

First Printing: December 2017
17 18 19 20 21 22 23   10 9 8 7 6 5 4 3 2 1
Printed in the United States of America

For:
Wesley Kawato
Nova Science Fiction
Marge and Dom
Zizi and Nunz

Special Thanks to Daniel Southern

Michael Edwin Q.

Dear Reader,

Submitted for your approval (or disapproval) is a collection of short stories. All of them are fabrications of my imagination, yet I've tried to weave a thread of truth through each one: that being the Christian point of view.

I realize this is unorthodox and I'm sure some will disapprove. Also, some will disagree with the way some of the topics are dealt with. My intentions were never to upset anyone, but to present the Word in a different light. My true intent was to put across Biblical teaching in an entertaining way. I've kept to what the Bible teaches, as far as I understand it. If at any point I've misinterpreted the true meaning, I'm sure I will be corrected in time.

I ask that you ignore whatever reviews may come, be they good or bad. Only you can decide.

If I can get people to read, think, and discuss, I feel I've succeeded. Never give up! Continue till there is no space between what you believe and who you are.

Blessings,

Michael Edwin Q.

Connect with the Author
michaeledwinq.com

Michael Edwin Q.

Stories

1

THE BLESSING

Two Roman guards led the prisoner down to the lowest cells of the prison. They held up the old man by his arms and yanked him to move faster. His sandals fell from his swollen feet as they hauled him down the stone staircase. The old man was thin and frail. His clothes were filthy and torn. His shoulder-length hair was white like ice. His wrinkled hands were scared from years of being gouged by fishhooks. His skin was tan from ten-thousand days under the blistering sun, cracked and weathered from as many nights exposed to the cold desert winds. Still, his eyes were as clear and bright as in his youth, learning the ways of fishermen from his father in their small boat on the Sea of Galilee.

The guards opened the grated-metal door and tossed him in. The old man fell down on his face.

"Here's your Rabbi," laughed one of the guards.

Two other prisoners rushed to help him to his feet. When he raised his head, they recognized him.

"Simon Peter, it's Simon Peter!"

Some fell to their knees before him.

"Stop it! Stop it! Get up! I've taught you better than that." He gestured for them to stand.

It was a large, dark, wet, stone cell, holding nearly fifty men, women, and children. All of them looked worn and hungry. Their eyes were wide and lit with the fire of fear.

"This is the day which the Lord has made; let us rejoice and be glad in it," the old man proclaimed. He tried to touch as many of them as he could. They held on to him for dear life, kissing his hands, tears streaming down their faces.

"Brothers and sisters, why wear such long faces? We are children of the living God and followers of Jesus, following the Way and walking in the light. Come; let us sing the hymns of our forefathers." He started them off in song, "I will praise the Lord who guides me: even at night my heart instructs me…"

Holding hands, they all began to sing, softly at first, then louder with more fervor; till all tears were dry and their faces glowed with new conviction.

Peter noticed an old man sitting alone; he smiled at Peter and nodded as if in recognition. Peter sat down next to him and placed his hand on his shoulder.

"Brother, it's good to see a smile that doesn't need coaxing to life." Peter looked into the man's smiling face. "I don't remember seeing you at the gatherings. Still, you look familiar. Do I know you?"

"We have met," the man said, "many years ago."

"We have? Tell me where."

"It was in Jerusalem."

"Then you speak true; it must have been many years ago." Peter examined the old man's face in what little light there was. "Forgive me, but I don't recall."

"We were both young at the time. You were a follower of our Lord, and I was a slave."

"You were a slave in Jerusalem. Tell me, in whose house?"

"It was the house of the High Priest, Caiaphas."

Peter's face became solemn; he stared into the man's eyes.

"Caiaphas! Then you were there?"

"Yes, I was there. It was difficult for Caiaphas to move freely among the commoners. Often, he sent me to follow Jesus and report to him what I saw and heard. I was his eyes and ears." The old man laughed, as if he told some private joke that Peter did not understand. The man continued.

"Yes, I was there. I was there when He spoke along the shores of Galilee. I was there when He fed the five thousand. I watched and listened when He spoke in the Temple. Yes, I was there.

"I would report it all in detail to Caiaphas. Then I would go to my room and lie awake each night, unable to sleep because of the words of our Savior echoing in my mind. All was so clear to me, but I would not accept Him. It went against all I knew before. My soul was dry from thirst, but I refused to drink. I just stared at the well but refused to bend my knee and partake.

"I prayed each night for a sign. Praise the Living God, one day I received it. You... you were the catalyst."

"Me?" Peter exclaimed.

"Yes, the Lord used you so I may see Him clearly."

"Brother, tell me, what is your name?"

"My name is Malchus."

Peter thought for a moment. "I'm sorry. I don't remember you."

Malchus took Peter's hand and placed it on the side of his face.

"You feel this ear? You were the one who cut it off."

Peter quickly withdrew his hand as if it were in the fire. "That night in the garden, when they arrested our Lord, I cut off your ear with my sword. Oh, my brother, please forgive me. I'm so sorry."

"I forgive you," Malchus smiled. "There is no need to feel sorry. If you had not cut off my ear, what followed may not have happened: a miracle."

Malchus stared forward into the darkness, as if seeing the past unfolding before his eyes.

"I remember that night as if it were last night. Caiaphas ordered me to go with the soldiers that I might see and bring him a full report later. We followed Judas through the garden till we came upon the Master. You were standing at His side.

"Someone said, 'Which one of you is Jesus?' He said, 'I am; and we fell to our knees, our bodies unable to withstand the power of His Word. Yet even then, after such a show of His authority, I was unwilling to accept Him.

"Suddenly, you jumped in front of Him to protect Him. You unsheathed your sword and began wheeling wildly at anyone and everyone. Praise to God, I was in the right place at the right moment in time. You sliced my ear clean off, and it fell to the ground at my feet.

"I remember: the Master rebuked you. He picked up my ear. I was holding the side of my head, the blood streaming down my arm. He took hold of my hand and moved it away from the wound. In the moment He touched me, calm like I never have known flooded me. He positioned the ear in place, and I was healed. At that instant, I knew who He was. I accepted Him and all that I ever heard Him say. I gave my life to Him and swore to follow Him all the days of my life and beyond. So, my brother, you see there is no need to apologize. I owe you so much."

"Tell me, what happened after that?" Peter asked.

"For many people, that was the end of the story; but for me, it was only the beginning. This healed ear was never the same. It hears what no others can. It hears the truth and only the truth. Whatever words it hears, even the lies of men, it knows only the truth. I listened as Caiaphas and the Pharisees told their lies, when they tried our Lord. Instead, I heard the truth in their words, how they hated Him and lied. I was there to hear you lie when you denied the Master three times. I knew your words were false; I heard the fear in your voice.

"All have sinned and fall short of the glory of God. All of us lie, Peter. I've only met one who didn't; and I stood at the foot of His cross and listened to His last words, my ear not needing to filter even one syllable.

"I heard the truth again, spoken by you to the many at Pentecost."

Malchus sighed before continuing. "Alas, the man who hears the falsehood in the words of other men becomes their enemy and the object of their hatred. Caiaphas became furious with me so he sold me for half my worth. That person sold me, and then that person sold me. I went from master to master.

I became the lead adviser to King Hereon of Canseco in the Far East. He never made a move unless I was at his side, deciphering the words of those around him. Word of his wisdom spread far and wide, but I guided him in court. He built me a palace adjoining his own nearly as grand as his. I lived like a king, but I was still a slave. When King Hereon died, I escaped. The truth will set you free; and I was free.

"These last few years I've spent spreading the good news. I always knew what to say because of this ear. You hear the words in your heart, and it echoes in your mind. The Spirit of God within you tells you what to say. As for me, I have been blessed; I hear Him whispering in this ear. His voice is sweet; it gives me comfort when all around me is chaos. It strengthens me when all else fails. His soft breathing comes to me at night and lulls me to sleep."

"Tell me, what do you hear now?" Peter asked.

"I hear the stomachs of starving lions growling for something to eat. I hear Nero's voice off in the distance saying he does not want you to die with us. You are to die alone; you are to face crucifixion."

"I will not have it," Peter demanded. "I am not worthy to die in such a manner, in the same way as our Lord."

Malchus stood and looked to the door of the cell. "I hear the guards coming for us. I hear the voice of the Master saying, 'Fear not, for I am with you always, even to the end of days!"

Just then, the cell door swung wide.

"It's time. Everyone out!" one of the guards shouted. "Except you," he said, pointing at Simon Peter.

Peter rushed to the door, touching each of them as they passed by and speaking to them. "Fear not, for He is with you. Sing my children; sing!"

They broke into songs of praise to the disbelief of the guards.

"These people are fools!" a guard announced.

"Or perhaps their God truly *is* God," another said to the stern look of his captain. Malchus was the last to leave.

"I will see you soon, my brother," Peter said, placing his hand on Malchus' shoulder.

"Yes, soon. Thank you again, Peter, for all you've done." He turned and began walking out. "Do you hear them, Peter? Do you hear the angels, the heavenly host signing, 'Glory to God in the highest heaven, and on earth, peace to those on whom His favor rests'?"

Peter listened intensely and smiled. "Yes, yes, Malchus, I hear them!"

THE END

2

THE STOWAWAY

The rain finally stopped. Listening, they all thought how unnaturally calm and quiet the animals were. The only sounds were the creaking wooden beams and the gentle slashing of the waves against the side of the ark.

Noah's wife let down her hair, preparing for sleep. "The first ten days of rain, I thought the sound would drive me mad," she said. "Yet now I don't know if I can sleep with all this quiet." Noah smiled at her, agreeing.

A knock at the door interrupted the peacefulness. Noah opened it to find his three sons: Shem, Ham, and Japheth.

Shem, the oldest, stepped forward. "Father, we are sorry to disturb you; but we believe something is wrong."

"What could be wrong, my son?" Noah replied. "Have not the rains stopped, and are not the animals quiet and peaceful?"

"Yes, Father; but it is the quiet that has brought this to our attention. At the ark's lowest level, where the grazing animals are, we heard a voice."

"What does this voice say?" Noah asked.

"First, it weeps aloud," Japheth replied, "then it calls out to its god for mercy, and again it weeps."

"Tell me, what is the name of the god this voice cries out to?"

Noah's third son, Ham, stepped up. "The voice cries, 'Oh great Minos, father of us all, have mercy on your son.' There is a moment of silence, and then again it weeps."

Noah took up his coat, looked at wife, turned, and walked past his three sons. "Come, my sons; have no fear. We must look into this." The ark's lowest level was a sea of horned beasts, cows, bulls, bison, water buffalo, and the like.

Hanging from the overhead beams were oil lamps swaying with the motion of the ship, causing shadows to spin and dance. Noah and his sons stood silent, listening.

The sound of weeping drifted out of the darkness, a voice cried out, "Oh great Minos, have I not suffered enough? Protect me and deliver me!"

Noah pounded down his staff. "Who is this Minos? Why do you pray to him for mercy? The one true God guides and rules this vessel. Who dares stowaway, hide in its belly, and pray to false gods?"

The voice went silent for only a moment. "Minos is no god. He is a man, but he is a powerful man. Minos has cursed me, and I've suffered since the day of my birth and will suffer till the end of my days." Again, the voice wept.

"Who are you?" Noah commanded. "Step into the light and show yourself."

A large, dark figure of a man slowly stepped into the light.

"Father!" Ham cried. "Look, father, this is no man! He is a beast! This creature is an abomination in the sight of the one true God! We should not allow it to remain! We must casted it out!"

"Is this the mercy of your God?" the stranger said. "You coddle all beasts great and small, yet you want to casted me out? True, I am not like you; but I am a man, nonetheless."

"You are no man, you are..."

"I will decide!" Noah shouted. "Tell me, my son, why do you say he is not a man?"

Ham looked the stranger up and down, "Because, I know his kind. They live in caves. They do not sow the land and eat of its fruit. They do not hunt or fish, but feast on the flesh of man."

"Is this true?" Noah asked.

"Yes, it is true; but if I am to be castaway for that, then so should half the beasts on this ark."

"True, but they are mere beasts," Noah said. "We are trying to decide if you are a man and worthy of mercy." Noah turned to Ham, "Continue, my son."

"It is not only his ways which are not human, just look at him. I've worked the land all my life. The sun's baked my skin dark. Yet, standing next to this creature, I am like the lilies in the fields. Look at his hair, if you may call it that. It's dark and burly, more like wool than hair. Look at his nose; it is wider than any natural man's. Its nostrils flare so large; you could easily place a metal ring there. Look at the top of his head. Surely that is the sign of Cain…"

"So what if he carries the sign of Cain on his head, which I doubt that is what it is!" Japheth interrupted. "Would that not mean that he is truly of the line of men? For was not Cain a man, like you and me? A murder? Yes. A sinner? Yes. Yet still, Cain was a man. Is it not written that God placed the sign on Cain that all men should know him, and that no harm should befall him from another?"

Japheth stepped forward. "I have listened to my brother, Ham, listing to all the reasons this stranger is a beast and not a man. Yet I look at him; and I see two legs and two feet, two arms and two hands. I look into his two eyes, and I see a soul. His voice speaks our language and cries for mercy. My heart goes out to him."

"My son, you have remained silent. What are your thoughts?" Noah asked his son, Shem.

"All of the beasts we have collected into this ark are those that God sent to us. They are of his choosing. If this stranger is a beast, as my brother Ham proclaims, then he is God-sent; in which case, we should not casted him out. If he is a man such as us, as my brother Japheth believes, then I cannot judge him; for I am no better."

Noah stepped in front of the stranger. "Who are you, stranger? Why and how are you here?"

"My name is Bufalus, son of Pasiphae. My people are hill people. We live in caves. Few others know of us, as we keep much to ourselves. For many seasons, I had a recurring dream. Every night, I dreamed of a great rain that would flood the world. One day, hiding in some tall grass, I listened to you speak to your people. I heard you warn them of the wrath of your God. They all turned their backs on you. I watched them laugh at you as you built this ark. I knew then that my dream would come true. I tried to warn my people; but like your own, they turned from me and laughed. Because I do not have a mate, I feared you would not grant me safe passage. So I stowed away and have hidden here since."

The three brothers stood silently waiting to hear their father's decision.

"Very well, you may remain," Noah said. The stranger nearly collapsed from relief. "Except, there are conditions you must remain to. You will labor for you passage. You will receive straw for a bed, and you will sleep here. Foremost, you will partake of only the grain and water we give you. This grain will be as meat to you, for you will not eat or harm any creature on this ark! Do you understand and agree to these terms?"

The stranger bowed in confirmation.

"Good," Noah said. "Now, come with me. There is something I must show you."

Noah walked past his sons with the stranger following close behind. They made their way up to the ark's next level, then the next, and the next, till finally they reached the top level. Noah walked over to a large cage, reached in and took hold of a dove.

"Come with me," Noah said, holding the dove to his chest. They walked up a flight of wooden stairs and entered a small room. The room was empty, save for a square wooden plank on the far wall. Noah slid the plank to one side, exposing an opening to the outside world.

The two walked up and looked out; it was a bright moonlit night.

"Water and air as far at the eye can see. Do you see those clouds? They are not hovering low as it may appear. It is we who've gone up to meet the clouds. Miles and miles of water are under us. The entire world is underwater, far below. Every place and everyone you have ever known are beneath us, covered with water." Noah looked to see his companion's reaction, but there was none.

Noah held the dove out the window and set it free, "If the bird cannot find a place to perch, he will return by morning. If he can find a place, he will not return. That will mean there is hope of dry land."

At that moment, the weight of Noah's statement found him. Tears began to roll down Bufalus's checks. Noah placed his hand on his shoulder, in sympathy.

"I have no mate!" Bufalus cried. "I am the last of my people! A noble race we were!"

"Tell me of your race. What was the name of your people?" Noah asked. "I have one son who calls you a beast and not a man; another son says you are different, but still a man. My third son will not say and leaves such matters in the hands of God. Tell me now the truth."

"The truth," Bufalus said with tears in his eyes, "I am neither beast nor man. I, Bufalus, last of my kind. I am the last minotaur."

Noah returned the wooden plank. The outside world disappeared.

THE END

3

THE PLEA

He hammers his fist on the old wooden door; he does this the correct amount of times in the correct rhythmic order. A peephole opens; a single eye stares at him.

"Who are you?"

"I am a child of Abraham." The passwords are correct. The door opens; he enters the darkness.

The guardian of the door holds up his lantern to get a better look at him. "It's you! What do you want?"

"I need to speak with Enos immediately; it's important!"

"Wait here; I'll see what he says." The guardian turns and heads down a long, dark tunnel. As he fades deep into the bowels of the earth, the light of his lantern grows smaller and smaller till it disappears.

As he enters the underground chamber, the guardian's eyes search for Enos. What little light there is, comes from the burning coals of a makeshift foundry in the center of the room. Its ruddy glow baths everything crimson. Some men shovel more coal on the dying embers and pump the bellows till they burst into flame, turning white-hot. Others hold the metal to the fire and, with iron mallets, pound it into the shapes of swords and spearheads.

The guardian greets Enos with a slight nod of the head. "Judas Iscariot is up top; he wants to see you. He says it's important."

"Tell him he's no longer welcome here!" snaps Nachum, second in command.

"No, wait," Enos says, grabbing the guardian's arm. "Bring him down." He turns to his comrades. "Let us hear what he has to say."

"Who is this Judas Iscariot?" asks one of the men.

"Just some fool," Nachum says. "He's a follower of some prophet named Jesus, as if Jerusalem doesn't have enough prophets. Only, this Jesus claims to be the Messiah. This Judas Iscariot came to us saying his master had great powers; he wanted us to be the muscle behind him when he took control of the city."

A man working one of the bellows stops and looks to Nachum, "Are you talking about the same Jesus who they arrested last night?"

"Yes," Nachum says. "He is the very same; and whom they've probably nailed to a tree and is dying even as we speak. 'Messiah'…what idiots we were to as much as listen to such nonsense. 'Save Israel'…the man can't even save himself."

The guardian escorts Judas into the chamber. Judas looks about the room desperately; he sees Enos and scurries to him. "Mercy, Enos, have mercy! Gather your men; we fight today for Israel, against injustice!" The grief-stricken man drops to his knees.

Enos looks down at the tormented Judas; he remains calm as he speaks. "Mercy…? You ask mercy for whom? From the time when the Lord cast our father Adam out of Eden till now, every living creature has cried for mercy. It is good such cries occurred over the course of so many years. If they were to cry out all at once, we would all go deaf."

Those standing about laugh at the idea; Enos smiles as he continues. "Injustice, you say. Which injustice are you talking about? The injustice of the Romans with their boot pressed down on our throats from generation through generation? Or perhaps, you speak of the Pharisees who go about in the temple making up laws as if each one of them were Moses? They make deals with the Romans, selling their brothers as Joseph's brothers did him!"

Enos turns to face those standing behind him. He smiles, shaking a single finger in the air as he makes his final point. "No…I know what injustice you speak about. It's the injustice to your leader who is bleeding to death on his cross this very moment. The mercy you ask for is for him. Well, it will never happen."

"As surely as God lives, he is innocent! You must save him!" Judas implores, his hands intertwined in a beggar's plea.

"Innocent!" Enos laughs as he whirls round. "He is not the first innocent man to suffer, nor will he be the last. If you think I would ask my men to lay down their lives for one innocent man, you're sorely mistaken!" Enos points his finger at Judas' face. "You said he had great power…he could walk on water….pull fish and loaves of bread out of thin air…heal the sick and raise the dead!"

"He is powerful," Judas pledges. "It's all true! I've seen it with my own eyes; I swear it!"

Enos snarls down at Judas, "You said if pushed to the edge, he would use his powers against the Romans. Well, you've pushed him past the edge, and all he can do is die. You promised a Messiah, but all you've delivered is an innocent man. You betrayed him; his blood is on your hands, now you want me to wash your sin away by attacking the Romans. It will never happen! It is your sin and his blood; both will remain on your soul forever!"

"No, don't say that!" Judas buries his face in his hands and cries.

"Get up off your knees, Judas; it makes me sick just looking at you."

Judas jumps to his feet, charging at Enos; he wraps both hands around Enos's throat, chocking him. "You fool," Judas shouts. "Don't you understand? He is the Messiah! We must save him! He mustn't die! This death must never occur! All will be lost! This death must never occur!"

The others seize Judas, pulling him from Enos and holding him back. Enos rubs the soreness from his throat; he balls his fist and is about to strike Judas, but then decides not to. He feels someone take hold of his arm and he turns to see who it is. It is the guardian of the door.

"What is it?" Enos roars.

"Symeon is here! He says he must speak with you. Life-and-death, he says."

"Then have him come in!"

"He did come; but when he stepped out of the tunnel, a look of fear came over him.

He ran back into the tunnel. He insists what he has to say is for your ears only. He waits for you in the tunnel."

Enos looks at the others, pointing at Judas. "Don't let go of him! Keep him here! I will return."

In the tunnel, Enos curses himself for not taking a lantern. His movements are slow and cautious. His footsteps on the stone walk echo all around.

A voice speaks a few feet in front of him. "Enos, is that you?"

In the dark, he can only see the outline of the man, a large dark shadow.

"Symeon, why didn't come to me?"

"I didn't want the others to hear. I don't want to start a panic."

"What do you mean…'panic'?"

"I've just come from outside the city. The one they called Jesus of Nazareth is dead."

"That is no surprise," Enos barks. "All those crucified die. Now, tell me what you mean when you say, 'panic.'"

Symeon continues in a whisper, "As I was making my way back to the city gate, I came on a small crowd of people huddled around an old, dried-away olive tree. It was obvious a man hung himself from the tree, and they were cutting him down. As I walked over, they placed the body on the ground; they were taking the noose from around his throat. I looked at the dead man; I recognized him straight away." Symeon hesitates.

"Go on," Enos orders. "Who was it?"

Symeon stammers, "It was….it was Judas Iscariot."

"That's impossible," Enos says, with a nervous laugh.

"No, Enos, I swear to you! It was Judas Iscariot."

A chill runs through Enos; the hairs on his body stand on edge.

"Then who is that we have with us below?"

Symeon is silent, afraid to answer. Enos turns and slowly returns to the foundry. His men are still holding tightly onto Judas. Enos stands before them. His knees bend, ready to jump in any direction at the first sign of danger.

He looks into the eyes of Judas and whispers, "Who are you?"

"You know who I am," Judas says, sounding remarkably calm, standing straight, and no longer fighting the men holding him. "You know me; I'm Judas Iscariot."

"No, you're not," Enos says. "Who are you?"

Judas resumes his struggling; the men tighten their grip on him.

"Why are you wasting time with foolish questions?" Judas shouts. "I tell you, he is the Messiah! We must save him! This death must not occur or all will be lost!"

"What will be lost?" Enos insists. "What will be lost?"

"You fool, he is the Messiah! All will be lost if we don't save him! This death must not occur!"

"Too late," Enos shouts. "I've just heard the word. Jesus of Nazareth is dead!"

Judas stops his struggling and stares at Enos. "You lie."

Enos looks at him coldly. "Jesus of Nazareth is dead."

Judas tilts his head to the ceiling, "Nooooooo!" he hollers like a wounded animal.

Without warning, Judas lifts his arms high; with the men still clinging to him, he tosses them off as if flinging away an uncomfortable silk shawl. The men fall many feet away, to all corners of the room.

They watch in horror as he transforms into his true self. His lips peel back, exposing gums and teeth. His teeth become long and sharp, as do his fingers and fingernails, like long, razor-sharp knives. His nostrils flare to twice their size. Red veins appear in his eyes and throb and bulge from his skull.

One of the men seizes a spear and hurls it at him. The beast catches it, breaking it like a twig.

"Fools: you're all fools! Do you realize what you've done?" the beast growls.

Nachum charges, sword in hand. The beast swats him aside as if swatting an insect. They all watch in terror as the beast walks into the fire and stands on top the white-hot coals. He raises his fist, shaking it in anger at heaven.

"You think because you've won, I'll give up; you're wrong! I will never give up! I don't care if I win! I do this because of my hatred of you! Curse you, Nazarene, curse you!"

In a flash of fire and smoke, he is gone. Only the sound of crackling embers do they hear. One by one, each man makes his way to his feet. They huddle close together, silent, afraid to speak. Enos takes a sliver of straw and places it on a hot coal, it catches fire. He uses the small flame to light one of the lanterns. Clutching the lantern at his side, he walks to the room's entrance.

"Enos," Nachum calls to him. Enos has one foot in the tunnel when he stops and turns. "Enos, where are you going?" Nachum asks.

There are tears forming in the eyes of Enos.

"I'm going to seek out the followers of this Jesus…this Jesus of Nazareth."

"Why?" Nachum asks.

The tears are now streaming down; his wet face reflects the glow of the dying coals.

"Don't you understand what this means?" Enos says softly. "The Messiah has come!"

He turns and disappears into the tunnel. Without speaking, each man in turn walks into the tunnel and follows, leaving everything behind.

THE END

4

THE WAIT

Katharine died well. One could even say her death was a joyous occasion. Nevertheless, please, don't misunderstand. This is not to imply anyone was happy to hear of her death or there were no tears shed at hearing of her passing. Every person whose life she touched loved her. She would be sorely missed. Yet still her passing they celebrated.

It was because Katharine lived many years. No one feels comfort when a young person passes on, least of all a child. But when someone has made it well up in years, such as Katharine, there can be feelings of acceptance, inevitability, and even relief.

The notion of dying in her own bed pleased Katharine, the same bed her husband died in many years earlier. As well, she had her closest friends and family gathered around her. Most important, seated at her bedside, smiling through the tears, holding her mother's hand, was her beloved daughter, Trisha.

The most noteworthy account of Katharine's passing is to say she died knowing the Lord. Twenty years earlier, she accepted Jesus Christ as her Savior; due in part to the persistent, gentle nudging of friends and family and lead by her daughter who had known the Lord since her teens.

Being right with the Lord and knowing her true and final destination: these allowed Katharine to find peace in letting go. At the moment of her death, Katharine found the transition from body to spirit an easy one. As easy as slipping off a pair of tight, hot shoes after a long, hard day and sliding your feet into a pair of soft, cool, wool-lined slippers.

Katharine suddenly realized she was floating along the ceiling and looking down at the proceedings. She saw an old woman lying motionless on the bed below; a young woman was shaking her.

"Oh, don't wake her!" Katharine cried down, "The poor old woman looks so tired; let her rest!"

Then the realization came to her; the old woman was her…or rather, what used to be her. Plus, strange as that prospect may sound, Katharine didn't feel the slightest confusion or fear.

In an instant, everyone and everything faded away; and she found herself engulfed in light. She followed its source till she found herself at the bottom of a grand, white, marble staircase. She started her way up and became aware of her movements, they were swift and easy. This was not the old woman's body she left behind. She could not guess at what her age was, not by the way she felt; there was no more stiffness or pain.

As she approached the top, there was more light; but this shone golden and warm. She saw standing at the top step, the figure of a man dressed in a long, white, flowing robe.

With each step forward, his features became visible. He was a young man, tall, with dark wavy hair and extraordinary good looks.

"Welcome, Katharine; we're so happy you've made it. All of heaven rejoices at your arrival!"

Reaching out both of his hands and taking hold of hers, he helped her up the few remaining steps. She felt the power in his arms.

Standing next of him, she could not take her eyes off his face, admiring his strikingly good looks.

"Are you Jesus?" she asked coyly.

His smile widened, exposing a full mouth of perfect, straight, white teeth. He chuckled slightly.

"No, I'm not," he said. "You will get to meet him soon enough; and you will have no question of whom he is. You'll know him when you see him."

Katharine was just about to ask, "Then who are you?" when he took hold of her hand and guided her from the steps. They came to a large gate made of shining gold; it was as tall as it was wide and stretched out in all directions beyond what you could see.

There was a large book resting on a wooden pedestal. He let go of her hand, walked over to the book, and opened it.

"This is the *Book of Life*," he proclaimed. "It's just a formality…We know your name is in it, but it needs announcing."

He thumbed through the book, stopped, and then pointed. Her gaze followed his finger to the middle of the page. There, written in golden letters, was her name.

Katharine looked up. She found herself drawn to the vague images passing behind the bars of the great gate. No longer interested in the *Book of Life*, she walked up close to the gate. She peered through the bars; but no matter how hard she squinted, all she saw was the motion of beautiful unearthly colors.

"Is it as grand as they say it is? Heaven, I mean," she asked as she took hold of two bars of the gate, trying to get a glimpse of something.

"I don't know," the young man said. "I've never been."

"What? You've never been?" Katharine cried as she let go and turned around. "I thought…I don't understand…why haven't you?"

He took hold of the *Book of Life* and rummaged a few pages back. He pointed.

"That is why!" he said sadly.

Again, her gaze followed his finger. There, near the bottom of the page, between two other names, was an empty slot.

"My parents never gave me a name," he whispered. "You cannot have your name written in the *Book of Life* if you don't have a name."

"Then, you'll never be able to…?" she asked.

"Oh, yes, someday. You see, I've waited so long; and I will have to wait even longer, perhaps till the End Times. I don't know."

A strange feeling came over Katharine as an even stranger notion came into her mind.

"I've heard it said, before someone enters heaven they're greeted by the person they have been the closest to on earth," she said.

"That's true," he replied.

"How can that be?" she pleaded.

He looked directly into her eyes.

Softly he responded, "Here…there is no one closer to you than I…we are of the same blood."

Katharine's thoughts began to race before her; and in a flash, it all became clear.

"When I was young," she said, "When I was young…foolish…unsaved and living my life without the Word…I had an abortion…" Her eyes widened with the realization. "I'm so sorry."

There were no words left to say. He said nothing, yet she knew it to be true. She reached up and took his face in her hands.

"I've always liked the name David. From now on, all will call you David."

She turned to look at the *Book of Life*. There, where an empty slot had been, was the name "David."

Tears began to flow from her eyes and from David's.

"I though there was no crying in heaven?" she said, smiling.

"There isn't," he replied. "We're not there yet…just a few more steps."

Suddenly, the gate opened wide; the two souls took hold of each other's hand and walked into heaven. As the gate closed behind them, David cried out, "Oh Mother, look! It's even grander than I imagined!"

THE END

5

THE TALE OF TWO CITIES

They secretly flew in four of the highest-ranking officers for the investigation. In a secure and guarded room, they sat at a long table. Their eyes focused on the lone soldier seated in the center of the room, facing the committee. The Senior Officer of the four addressed him.

"Major Gilmore, understand this committee is here only to collect all the information about the incident so we can form a conclusion. Understand, this not a court. We are not here to judge you; but if you refuse to cooperate, that forces us to consider other alternatives."

Major Gilmore sat silently. The committee leader handed out papers to all the others and began to read from his copy.

"On March 28, 1951, you, Major Gilmore, were leader of a small squad ordered to fly over Niche-Ho, a tiny island in the South Pacific, and drop an atomic bomb on it. It was an uninhabited island. The purpose of the mission was to see if a small crew could deliver such a payload. It was you, Major Gilmore, as pilot and leader; Major Taft was copilot; Captain Moore was the navigator; and Captain Hernandez was the bombardier.

"According to all records, the mission was going just fine, when suddenly your plane disappeared from the radar screen; and there were no visuals or radio communication. It was as if you vanished into thin air. After an hour, you reappeared on radar as mysteriously as you vanished, only minus the bomb. The Island of Niche-Ho remained unharmed.

"We've talked to the others, and they are as mute as you. Now you, sir, being the one in charge, I'm afraid you must shoulder all the responsibility. I order you to tell us what happened."

Major Gilmore squirmed in his seat, avoiding all eye contact.

Another member of the committee spoke up. "Major Gilmore, a missing atomic bomb is..." He searched for words. "I don't need to tell you how important this is. There's so much at stake. You must tell us what happened. If you don't care what happens to you, think of the others. All of them have families. Must they spend years in prison because you won't do your duty?"

Major Gilmore's voice was small and frightened. "It's not that I don't want to cooperate. It's just that I'm afraid you'll think we've all gone mad. What happened that day was impossible, but it did happen."

"Go ahead, Major, we'll take what you've said into consideration. Please, continue."

"Well, it started out like any other mission, even though it was such a small crew. We took off on schedule, radio communications were clear, and all systems were go. I sat in my place; copilot Major Taft sat next to me; navigator Captain Moore sat behind us with his charts; and Captain Hernandez, the bombardier, was away from us in the belly of the ship. When we reached our planned altitude, the radio went on the fritz. It began sputtering; hissing, whistling, and then it went dead. Taft and I looked at each other; and before anyone could say another word, they appeared."

"'They appeared', you say," one of the officers asked. "Who is this 'they'?"

Gilmore hesitated and then continued. "They were men, sir. There were four men, one standing near each of us and holding guns to our heads."

An officer jumped up in protest. "I'm not going to sit here and let him insult us with some fairy tale!"

"Sit down, General; I want to hear this," Number One said. "Continue, Major."

"They wore uniforms, old-time pilot's outfits. You know; leather jackets with thick, wool collars; shiny, black leather boots to the knees, the works. Also, when they spoke, we could hear them in our headphones."

Another officer interrupted. "What did they look like? Did they wear any insignia? What country were they from?"

"There was no way of telling," Gilmore replied. "Also, as impossible as this all sounds, there is something else, something even stranger." He hesitated for a longtime. "They all looked like movie stars."

"What?" an officer shouted.

"I know it sounds crazy, sir; but they each looked like a famous movie star. The man next to me was Clark Gable, the one behind Tate was Spencer Tracy, and Henry Fonda held a gun to Moore's head. Though we couldn't see Hernandez down in the weapons bay, we learned that he was the captive of Jimmy Stewart."

"Do we have to sit here and listen to this insanity?" barked an officer. Number One held up his hand for him to be silent. He nodded to Gilmore to continue.

"Clark Gable seemed to be the one in charge. He ordered us to fly straight into the cloud in front of us. Entering the cloud, all conditions changed. We were in a terrible storm. Lightning and thunder tossed us around, bolts of electricity danced over the ship. I felt us increase speed. I looked at the panel: all gages were at zero. Finally, we came out of the cloud. We slowed down to normal speed. I looked down. We were over a desert. Henry Fonda pushed Moore aside, took a map from his jacket, and gave me flight instructions. Everyone remained silent. Then suddenly, the four strangers began arguing."

"About what?" Number One asked.

"Well, it seems Spencer Tracy was upset with Clark Gable. He called him Gabe. He said, 'Gabe, I don't see why you always get to be Clark Gable. Next time, why don't you be Tracy, and I'll be Gable.' Then Henry Fonda butt in. 'Tell me, how did I get to be Fonda? He's a great actor and all, but I'd rather be someone dashing like Errol Flynn or Douglas Fairbanks.' 'Junior or Senior?' asked Tracy. 'Does it matter?' replied Fonda.

"Though we couldn't see him, we heard Jimmy Stewart's voice coming from down below in our headsets. 'What about me? I've got to talk like I've got marbles in my mouth. I'd rather be a British actor who speaks well, like Lawrence Olivier.'

"This bickering went on for ten or fifteen minutes till Fonda looked up and stopped everything short. 'Shut up, you guys; we're there!' he shouted. Gable gave Stewart the order, 'Bombs away!' Only Hernandez wouldn't do it. Stewart pressed his gun against Hernandez's head. 'If you've seen any of my westerns, you know I'm a crack shot, and at this range, I never miss.'

"Gable pressed his gun against my head. I spoke into my mouthpiece, 'Go ahead, Hernandez, let her go.' They immediately ordered us to turn around. We headed back into the cloud we came from. Just as we entered it, we felt the bomb's blast. Once in the center of the cloud, all was still. Then the storm and electricity started again. Minutes later, we're out of the cloud and at the exact position we started in.

"Gable had us turn and face him. 'A job well done, gentlemen', he said. 'Sorry for the inconvenience. Just remember, movies are your most reasonably priced form of entertainment.' He, Tracy, and Fonda, broke into laugher. We could hear Stewart laughing in our earphones. Then Gable smiled at me. 'Thank you, again. Blessings on all of you.' Then in the blink of an eye, they all vanished.

"Instantly, we had radio contact; we were back on the radar. After we landed, before we left the ship, I took the map Fonda used, and slipped it in my jacket. Here it is. It will explain everything."

Major Gilmore walked over and placed the map on the table. The officers gathered around and examined it.

"I recognize this terrain. It's a desert area in the Middle East," said an officer.

"What is this here?" Number One asked.

"That was our drop site," Gilmore replied.

"What does it say here," Number One said, taking up a magnifying glass. He read the name of ground zero. "Sodom and Gomorrah?" They all looked at Major Gilmore in bewilderment.

"I told you that you'd think we'd all gone mad." He turned, sat down, and placed his face in his hands.

THE END

6

THE END TIMES

Every payday, I like to treat myself to a cold one. Normally, I go to Max's with the guys or to the Clipper to play pool; but that day I was thirsty, more thirsty than usual. We cooked the entire day out on the loading dock. There wasn't a breeze for miles, and dust that once settled on boxes in the warehouse lodged in the back of my throat. I was thirstier than usual, thirsty enough to stop at the nearest bar, the Dewdrop Inn. I don't much like the Dewdrop. It's small, dark, and usually empty; but a cold one was all that mattered.

Once my eyes adjusted to the dark, I sat down at the bar. The sound was off on the television; there was an unplugged jukebox against the back wall that looked like it hadn't seen use in years. The bartender at the far end of the bar was on a stool, doing a crossword. There was one lone customer, an old man staring at the beer bottle in front of him.

I rapped my knuckles on the bar to get the bartender's attention.

"Yeah, what can I do for you?"

After serving me a draft, he went back to his crossword.

I eyed the old guy sitting across from me. He looked ancient. What few strands of hair that still clung to his scalp were white as snow, as were the whiskers covering his jaw from one ear to the other. He was thin; he swam in the ragged old clothes on his back. It was clear he had drunk heavily for many years. When he put the beer bottle to his mouth, it was hard to tell who was sucking on whom harder.

I held my glass in toasting fashion. "How's it going old-timer?"

He looked at the beer bottle in front of him, ignoring me.

I was ready to down my drink and get out of there when I heard him speak.

"I'm sorry, are you talking to me?"

"Yes, I was," I said.

"I'm sorry; my hearing's not what it used to be."

"No sweat. What are you drinking?"

"Beer, mostly."

"Two more…one for my friend here, and one for me," I announced to the bartender.

I moved over and sat next to him.

"So…how's it going?" I asked.

"It just goes," he replied as he took hold of his new beer.

"You retired?"

"I guess you could say that."

"Guess…? Why, what did you used to do?"

"If I told you, you'd think I was crazy," he said. "You'd think I was some crazy old drunk, that I am; and you would politely excuse yourself and go sit back down over there."

"No I won't. Go ahead, try me."

"All right, I will," he said; and then he took another long draw from his beer. He placed the bottle down. "I used to be an angel," he said, looking me square in the eye.

He was right; I did feel an urge to get up and politely make my way back to my seat at the far end of the bar.

"Ya see, I said you would think I was crazy," he said.

"Now, did I say that? You just took me off guard, that's all; but you left me with a million questions!"

"Go ahead; ask."

"When you say angel…do you mean the kind with wings and harps?"

"That's a far-fetched stereotype, but I guess my answer would have to be 'yes.'"

"If that's true, what the heck are you doing drinking in a downtown bar?"

"It's a long story," he said.

"Oh no, you don't," I said. "Long story or not, I want to hear this!"

We each took a long hit from our beers. He continued.

"Ok, here it goes. Many years ago…"

"How many years ago?" I interrupted.

He chuckled at my stupidity. "Before you came into being, before anything was, we were all in heaven."

"Who…who is we?" I interrupted again.

He looked at me, a bit disturbed at the interruption. "The angels! God and the angels were in heaven. Gee, don't you ever read the Bible?"

"Not lately."

"It would seem so," he decided. He continued. "Anyways, we were all in heaven, each with his specific duty. Well, Lucifer, the head angel…"

"I've heard of him," I interjected.

"That's nice," he said, clearly patronizing me. "Anyways, Lucifer grew tired of being only first mate and decided to have a mutiny. He started a campaign against God and many of us followed. He made promises to us he could never deliver, but the temptation was great."

"What were you thinking? I mean, going against God and all…he's God, right?" I asked.

"It sounded like a good idea at the time," he said sourly. "Anyways, we found ourselves cast out of heaven and sent to earth. In fact, it seemed like it was all going to work out just fine. I mean, we were in charge of the earth, and you humans are so easily swayed. It all seemed like nothing could stop us, and we would win. Then, *he* came."

"Who came?" I asked.

"You know, I'd rather not say his name."

"You mean…"

"Yes, *him*…He changed the whole enchilada."

"I still don't understand what you're doing drinking beer in a downtown bar?"

"I grew old," he said. "So they retired me."

"I didn't know angels aged," I said.

"Just fallen ones; and even they age at different rates. I was just one of the unlucky ones who age quickest."

"That still doesn't answer what you're doing in a downtown bar."

"Where else can I go?" he asked sadly. "Lucifer put me out to pasture; I can't put my tail between my legs and go back to heaven."

"Why not?" I said.

"I just can't," he replied. "You don't understand what waits for me there."

"Ah...eternal punishment?" I asked.

"No, it's something worse than that. It's love...love and forgiveness. I couldn't live with that."

"You couldn't....I don't understand."

"Of course you can't; you're human." He finished his beer. "I have no place to go. So I sit here in a downtown bar waiting for the end times."

"Yeah, but that could take forever," I said. "This bar will probably be long gone before then."

He pointed to the silent television anchored from the ceiling over the bar.

"Just look at the news; things have never been so horrible. Do you honestly think the end is far away? No, this is the last bar I will have to spend my time in; but I'm not worried. When we get close to the end, Lucifer will need all hands on deck. There'll be a place for me again, I'm sure."

"Yeah, but you'll lose!" I insisted.

"Look who's talking! 'Do you read the bible?' 'Not lately,' he says. Wasting all your money and time in bars...ask the bartender for some eternal salvation...think he keeps some stashed behind the bar? You big dope!"

The old man shouted at the bartender, "Say, Jimmy, you got any salvation in the backroom?" Jimmy chalked it up as the ravings of an old drunk and continued with his crosswords, ignoring him.

The old man turned on his stool and faced me.

"He's God…how can you go against God?' he asks. You big dope, you do it your entire life, and no one jumps on *your* case!

"You'll lose,' he says. You're as lost as I am, you big dope! Of course we'll lose, but who cares? Have you eve read Milton?"

"Milton?" I asked.

"I thought not," he said, shaking his head. "It doesn't matter. They'll call me up to the front soon enough. Till then, I'll just sit here drinking." He looked at his empty beer bottle and then at me with expectation. I ordered him another beer.

"Hadn't you better be getting home to the wife and kids?" he asked, not looking at me.

"I don't have a wife or kids," I answered.

"That's what I'm saying, 'hadn't you better be getting to the wife and kids'; while there's still time; and there's so little time!"

I backed away from him slowly toward the door. If he was telling the truth or if he was crazy as a June bug, it didn't matter; he scared me to death.

I never went back to the Dewdrop Inn; but for the next year, each day after work I walked by and looked inside through the window. The old man was always there, seated on his usual stool, sucking on his bottle of beer.

Only reason I've mentioned this to you now is because…last payday, I looked through the window of the Dewdrop Inn; the old man wasn't there.

THE END

7

THE MAN WHO KILLED GOD

I cannot say with any certainty when he first appeared; I only remember I was young, perhaps three or four. His appearance remained the same throughout the years: long, white hair with matching waist-length beard; full-length white robe; brown sandals; porcelain-white skin; and sky-blue eyes. His voice was more like a soothing hum in my mind, yet I understood every word.

I remember his first words, "Love me with all your heart, mind, and soul. Love me." It seemed like a good idea at the time; so I did.

As years passed, he began making demands of me, small ones, at first. To be honest, what he asked of me made all the sense in the world to me. "If you love me, you will obey me," he often said. Laws that exalted him, created order in the world, and made a better person of me.

The next step was only natural. "If you love me, you will worship me."

"Of course," I cried, "but how?"

"Fall to your knees and pray!"

He taught me the words and the order they're spoken in. I fell to my knees and recited them over and over. I spoke them when I wanted to praise and adore him. I spoke them when I wanted something to happen or for something not to happen. I recited them for me and others, even my enemies.

"The more you pray, the greater the worship and the greater the reward." The reward he spoke of, he called heaven.

One day, he said, "Love me, and love the saints."

"Who are the saints?" I asked.

"Those souls whom I have chosen," he said.

So I learned new prayers – prayers to the chosen.

I can only say that his next request seemingly made even more sense than his demand to pray to the saints.

"To love the father, you must love the son. You get to the father through the son but you get to the son through the mother." I learned to pray to her. I recited the prayer day and night.

"How much and how often do you pray?" he asked.

I had no idea, no answer.

"Here are beads to help you keep track."

I ran my fingers across the beads; I tried my best.

"You know, you're a hopeless sinner," he said.

"I know," I said, "but what am I to do?"

He placed me in a large wooden box. I sat there in the darkness until a small window opened. A man sitting behind a veil spoke softly, "Speak your sins, my son."

"My sins," I cried. "What has this man to do with my sins?"

The words hummed in my mind, "He's no ordinary man; he speaks for me."

"Where does it say that?" I shouted, holding up the Bible.

"What are you doing reading that? You, with your limited mind; put that away! Only the man behind the veil can interpret it correctly. Now stop this foolishness and tell him your sins."

I did just that; I told him my sins, even my most intimate thoughts. For my penance they gave me prayers to say, mostly those to the chosen ones and his mother. After this and an act of contrition, I found myself in what they told me was a state of grace. The benefits of which allowed me freely to take part in any of the sacraments, one being permission to drink his blood and eat his flesh. Though it looked much like common bread and wine, they told me looks can be deceiving. It, in fact, was his blood and flesh.

Another sacrament bestowed to me was matrimony. In my mid-twenties, I married the love of my life. This union produced two beautiful, healthy baby boys. As good servants, we had both children baptized days after their birth.

"Why must we baptize them so young?" I asked.

"To wash away all trace of Original Sin," he answered.

"That's true, but shouldn't that be their choice when they're at an age to make their own decisions?"

"Have you been reading the Bible without proper guidance again?" he asked.

"No, I was just thinking that…"

"Stop thinking!" he demanded. "If you were supposed to think, you'd have a larger, perfected brain. That's why there are groups of the earthly chosen to do the thinking for you. Stop thinking!"

"Sorry," I said shyly.

"Sheep don't tell the shepherd the best place to graze!"

"I'm sorry," I repeated.

***

The years did what years do: they slipped away. I was what we call middle-aged. It was now just my wife and me. The boys had grown up and gone off to start families of their own. We had taught them well. They followed the rules as closely as we did, and I though that was why he appeared so seldom. As long as we followed the rules, I heard little from him. Only when there was an infraction or bending of a law, a misdemeanor by me or a family member did his words come humming into my brain. I received appearances brought on by gross infringements, felonies to the law. Still, I'm proud to say these were few and far between. What sustained me mostly was encouragement and advice from the earthly chosen ones; especially, the counsel given during my weekly visits to the large wooden box.

***

They told me his ways were strange and mysterious, but I never thought much about it until the strangeness touched me personally. It came in the form of a phone call, a phone call my wife and I expected with great anticipation. It was to be the announcement of the birth of our first grandchild, but it was a declaration of sorrow. The child was stillborn.

I ran to the large wooden box for answers.

"He does work in..."

"In mysterious ways! Yes, I know that!" I shouted. "Yeah, but that isn't an answer! That doesn't stop the pain!"

The lumpy cassock on the other side of the veil slumped in his chair and remained silent.

"Well, there's at least one comfort," I whispered. "At least the child is in heaven."

"Surely, that he will be...someday," the lump murmured.

"Someday...what do you mean someday? The child was innocent!"

"That is true, my son. Which is why he is worthy of heaven; and someday he will enter it. Understand, my son, the child never received baptism. He must wait till the end of this age."

"Are you telling me that if I were to die tomorrow, I would not find my grandchild in heaven?"

"My son, if you were to die tomorrow, what makes you think you would go to heaven?"

"I've confessed my sins!"

"Yes, but if you were to sin between now and then, you lose the grace you earned today."

"I'm just a man...I sin every day!"

"The best you can hope for is a stay in purgatory."

Fear and anger took hold of me. I ran out of the wooden box. I ran passed the streets and houses. I ran passed forests, rivers, and valleys. I ran to the top of the mountain and shook my fist at the sky.

"Come down here, old man; I want to talk with you!" I hollered.

I blinked, and he stood before me. His humming words in my brain, "What do you want of me, my son?"

"Don't call me your son! I'm nothing to you, and you're nothing to me, nothing, you understand! You're useless, old man. You and your laws and rules...you're useless! I want nothing to do with you ever again!"

He walked up to me with a smug smile. "Do you know who you're talking to? Do you know what I could do to you?" He gestured his hands, palms up, in a questioning motion. "What's it going to be, boy? Both your parents are still living. How about a tumor the size of a baseball in your mother's brain to leave her in pain the rest of her years? Or maybe a stroke on your father's right side, and then you can listen to his mumbling as you daub the spittle from his mouth?" His hand closed into fists. "You've still two strong sons. If I struck them blind, you could buy them pencils to sell on the corner." Then his smile grew larger. "That beautiful wife of yours…I wonder what she'd look like with both breasts lost to cancer?" He shook his head and raised his fists to my face. "There's a lot I can do. You have no idea who you're messing with, boy."

I jumped at him and wrapped my hands tightly around his throat. He fell to his knees, choking; the humming of his voice left my brain.

"I want nothing to do with you, old man. I want you to leave me and my family alone. The bond between us I claim broken forever!"

I gripped tighter as he gasped for air; and like a puff of smoke, he disappeared. The world went dark. All I saw were the stars of the night above me. I sensed the presence of something all around, of something new and unknown to me.

"Who is there?" My voice trembled.

In my mind I heard a calm and gentle voice, "I am that I am."

"Is it you I should love with all my mind, heart, and soul?" I asked.

"That will come in time," He said. "First, let Me tell you how much I love you."

THE END

8

THE VOICE OF GOD

Slowly, the great gates of Candor opened. Four teams of six mighty Ogle beasts, with nostrils flaring and haunches burning moved the massive barrier. The air, electric; all around silence until Tyron stepped out from the mammoth arch and into view. The crowd waited so long for just a glimpse of him. When he marched into the light, they roared. They threw flowers at his feet. At the end of the Avenue of Heroes, he climbed the 139 steps up to the Palace of Light.

At the top, he entered. Behind closed doors, the cheers sounded muffled and faraway. Two Chaulmoogra priests greeted him. Having taken a vow of silence, they used hand gestures, begging him to follow. They passed through the Hall of Flames; red embers lined the walkway. A thin ferromagnetic membrane protected them from the heat. They walked through the Hall of Waters with its dancing fountains in lucent ponds supplied by waterfalls. Multicolored Tremble Fish jumped from pool to pool, part of their playful mating ritual.

Entering the Hall of Law and Truth, a sea of courtiers parted, allowing him to approach the High Ruler seated on his throne. The High Ruler stood up and threw his arms out far.

"All hail our returning hero, Tyron!"

"Hail Tyron!" they sang in unison.

The High Ruler raised his hands. "For three long ages, Tyron remained on distant soil, a planet far off in the galaxy of Bureaus. He watched, studied, and collected data. He returns now a wiser man.

Tell us, Tyron; tell us of this other world we see in the night sky." The Ruler again sat; the hall went silent. Tyron stepped forward, bowed to all, and spoke.

"Oh, Great Mistaya, ruler of all, three long ages I remained among strangers. I saw many wonders, and returned with a vast collection of knowledge and wealth from this strange planet. They are good people there, for the most part, with many likenesses to us, but even more differences. I will show you."

A large videogenic screen on the far wall went bright. Pictures of a blue-white planet appeared.

"Behold the planet Earth!"

Chattering flew through the hall, then again silence.

"This was our view as we approached the planet." Scenes flashed on the screen. "This is a map showing divisions between different peoples. They call them Countries. This is how they see their world: in fragments."

The Ruler interjected, "I studied Topography as a child; and I see lands, oceans, rivers, and mountains; and you tell us those lines are self-inflicted borders? Tell me, what is the purpose of separating the land into…what did you call them? Countries?"

"Each Country is different from the others, as are the peoples. They have different customs, different governments, dress, food, and even different languages."

"With different customs and languages, how is their Ruler able to reign in truth and wisdom?"

"There is no one Ruler, Sire. Each Country has its own Ruler."

Laughter echoed throughout the hall.

"Surely that can only lead to Chaos!" the High Ruler exclaimed.

"That is true, Highness: they live in constant chaos. I found it unbearable. Each inhabitant swears loyalty to their own Ruler, and then tries to impose their laws and way of life on other countries!"

The Great Ruler sat forward on his throne. "What is the purpose of imposing your ways on others?"

"During all my time spent there, this point was never clear to me."

"Perhaps, Tyron, each feels their way to be superior. So acting in love, they try to lead others into their ways."

"One would only hope so, Highness; but I found the opposite to be true. They impose on the other for gain, for profit. I found no love or caring in it. Each Ruler is untrusting of the other, even to the point of hatred. And his people follow suit in this anger. Sometimes this mistrust and hatred grows so great that they do the strangest of things. They call it 'War.'"

"Explain to me what this 'War' is. Does it relieve them of their mistrust and hatred of one another?"

"On the contrary, Sire, it inflames it. War is conflict."

"A contest!" the High Ruler shouted in excitement. "Well, at least this sounds civilized."

"No, Highness, it is conflict to its worst end. Not just a contest of strength and cunning, each group of peoples does whatever it can to destroy the other group."

"You mean a contest to the death?"

"Yes, Highness, it's called 'Combat'; and it is to the death."

Gantt, the High Priest of the Samara Order stepped forward.

"The priests, Tyron. Where are the priests during this madness? This is a path away from wisdom. Surely they advised these people to give up such insanity?"

"One would think so, but not always. Though some priests warn against such actions, others sanction it."

"How is that possible?" Gantt declared. "How can one priest think differently from another? The truth is the truth; the path is the path."

"Honorable Gantt, you speak rightly. Yet on 'Earth' they live by different truths and different paths. This difference, sometimes, is the very cause of War."

"Then I pity them. I ask all priests of the Samara and Chaulmoogra orders to keep them in their prayers."

"Prayer!" Tyron shouted. "Prayer is the reason I stayed so long on this planet.

For what is prayer? Is it not when your thoughts blend with those of your God? This is so with us, but even more so with those of Earth."

"What are you saying?" Gantt asked.

"I'm saying these people of Earth may be pitiful, but they are blessed with a gift we can only dream of. They have a process by which they can receive messages from God and literally hear Him, the very Voice of God!"

"How can that be? It is impossible!"

"I agree," Tyron claimed. "I find it disturbing that God would speak directly to a race of beings so far from the path, but He does. I spent ages on this planet studying the method they use. I tell you, today all of you will hear the voice of God!"

Tryon gestured to the guards, and the doors to the hall opened. Attendants wheeled in a large dark box. It was black in color with a smooth mirror-like surface. At one end of the black box were a series of levers.

"Before we start," Tyron announced, "let me explain the process. God speaks to one person, softly and silently in their mind. That person puts down the word of God on paper in a sacred code." Tyron holds up a large piece of paper with lines, dots, and dashes on it. "Anyone trained in the reading of such messages, can run the code through this black box; and out will come the voice of God."

All waited silently to hear what would come next.

Tyron sat down before the black box, placed the message down, and began to work the levers.

The room became filled with a strange sound; it echoed off the walls and ceiling. It was a sound so magnificent and beautiful, inwardly you did not want it to ever stop; but you knew if it continued, it would kill you.

Tryon finished working the last of the message through the black box. Men stood like statues, women shook, rows of Samara priests fell to their knees. All wept, uncontrollable crying.

The High Ruler stepped forward and announced, "Truly, this day we have heard the Voice of God! Tyron, tell us the name of this method."

"They call it 'Music', Highness," Tyron proclaimed. "And this machine they call a Piano, and the prayer we have heard, they called 'Clare de Lune.'"

The High Ruler, still crying, wiped the wetness off his checks. "What is this?" he asked holding his moistened palm to Tyron.

"It is nothing to worry about, Sire; it will not harm you. The people of Earth call them 'Tears.'"

THE END

9

WHAT WERE YOU THINKING

She kicks open the door to her office, violently; so much so it nearly swings back and hits her in the face. She takes hold of the door, and this time opens it slowly till it stops fully ajar.

In all her years as principal of M. H. Sanger High School, never has she faced anything that angered her as much as this has. The homecoming dance was always a night of excitement and celebration for students and faculty alike. Only now, the night seems ruined, all because of this...incident.

Principal Elaine Peters enters her office followed by the two offending students: Christopher Powell and Mary Ella Barton. Because of the late hour, the office is dark; Principal Peters turns on her desk lamp. The light casts down brightly on her desktop, but it is scarcely enough to light up the rest of the office. She doesn't want to turn on the overhead light. If the News Media catch wind of the goings-on at the homecoming dance, there are sure to be News cameras outside the school. If they see light coming from her office window they'll know for certain where she is. She wants to get through this with as little publicity as possible.

"You...you sit over there," she orders Mary Ella, pointing to the brown leather couch pressing against the far wall, away from the windows. "And you...you sit in that chair," she commands Christopher, pointing to a matching brown leather chair on the opposite end of the room, far from Mary Ella. "Now the two of you just sit here! I don't want either one of you to get up from your seat! I don't want you to talk. No talking. You understand? Silence! I'm going in the other room to call both your parents. I will be right back. Remember, not a peep from either one of you!"

Principal Peters dashes out. She slams the door behind her; the glass panel in the door with her name and title written on it nearly shakes out of place. A light goes on in the outer office. Through slits in the Venetian blinds covering Principal Peters' office windows, they see her sitting at a desk and dialing a phone.

Christopher and Mary Ella sit for a moment in silence. He is a handsome dark-haired boy. He has just turned eighteen that month; a year and a month older than Mary Ella. He has on a black tuxedo with satin lapels and strips running down the sides of his pants. Under his jacket, he wears a white ruffled shirt with a black velvet bowtie. In his lapel buttonhole is an overlarge, bright-yellow sunflower that is absolutely comical. He knows it looks silly, which is why he chose to wear it.

Mary Ella is a sandy-blonde-haired, light-skinned beauty. Physically mature for her young age, she wears a lime-green satin evening gown that flows to the ground and is held up at the top by thin spaghetti straps. She's done her hair up high; a string of fake pearls dangle from the back of her neck and down onto the front of her gown. There is a white orchid pinned just above her right breast.

"I'm sorry," Christopher says, breaking the silence.

"Well, I'm not," Mary Ella remarks. "I'm glad we did it. I thought you'd be too."

"I am," Christopher replies. "I'm just sorry I got you mixed up in something like this."

"Don't be silly," Mary Ella says. "It was just as much my idea as it was yours."

They return to silence, trying to listen in on Principal Peters' phone conversations in the outer office.

"That's right, Mr. Powell; your son, Christopher, is here in my office right now. Well, I'd prefer not to say over the phone; it's of a rather delicate nature," Principal Peters' voice trails off as she listens to the concerns of Christopher's father.

"I understand…I understand…" Peters' head bobs up and down agreeing with every word spoken on the other end of the line.

"Well, if you must know…" She cups her hand over the phone receiver and whispers into it, as if relaying a top-secret message. Christopher and Mary Ella can't make out what she is saying.

"What do you think they'll do to us?" Mary Ella asks, her voice emitting the full weight of her concern.

"I don't know…shoot us at sunrise?" Christopher's humor is lost in the moment.

"I wish they would," Mary Ella says. "I'd rather face a firing squad than my parents. They'll probably ground me for a whole year."

"A year…is that all?" Christopher scoffs. "My folks will probably ground me for life!"

Just then, Principal Peters flies into the room; she faces the two of them, leans against the front of her desk, and rests her hands on the edge of the desktop.

"Well, I've contacted your parents; and they're on they're way."

She goes silent for a moment and gazes back and forth, first at Christopher, then at Mary Ella, and then back at Christopher.

"What were you thinking?" she asks, not directing her question to either one of them in particular. "Did you think it would be funny…some kind of joke?" She continues, "I mean…you're both not serious about all this?"

Neither of the two students answer; they just look across the room into each other's eyes. There is a look of sorrow on both of their faces; but as if some unspoken words have communicated between the two of them, they begin to smile at each other.

"I don't believe it!" Principal Peters exclaims. "You are serious, aren't you? Well, I never! This puts a new light on everything. I don't know what we're going to do with you two!"

Principal Peters goes silent again; the boy and girl speak not a word. The three remain quiet in the dimly lit office for what feels like an eternity. Finally, a knock on the door shatters the stillness.

"Yes, who is it?" Principal Peters poses her question to the door.

"Tom Powell…I'm Christopher's father?"

"Yes, come in, Mr. Powell," Principal Peters stands up straight and backs away from her desk.

The two greet each other with a handshake.

"Sorry to get you out here in the middle of the night, Mr. Powell," Principal Peters apologizes, "but you can understand my concern?"

"No, I don't understand," Tom says. "Christopher has never been one for causing any problems. What's the big deal? So two kids decided to play a prank on their classmates. It was just a harmless joke, right?"

"No, Mr. Powell, it's not some harmless joke. It would seem these two are quite serious about what they did," Peters remarks.

Tom looks at Mary Ella, and then he turns to Christopher, "Nah, that can't be true. Christopher, tell Principal Peters you were just joking around." He looks straight at Christopher, but the boy shamefully stares silently at the floor.

Before anyone says another word, Pat Barton, Mary Ella's mother, rushes into the room. She ignores all greeting formalities and walks passed everyone till she stands in front of her daughter.

"Where did you get that ridiculous…?" She takes a moment, searching for just the right word. "…Costume?"

"In a Goodwill store; I think it's pretty," Mary Ella says soulfully.

"Well, I think it makes you look cheap!" her mother bellows.

"Ms. Barton, please!" Principal Peters demands.

"I suppose this is the boy?" Pat Barton turns and points at Christopher. The boy is still silently staring a hole in the floor.

"Ms. Barton, I'm Tom Powell; I'm Christopher's father." Tom thinks it best to make the first move. He reaches out his hand to Pat in greeting; she ignores the gesture.

"Well…Mr. Powell…I don't know how you've raised your boy; but we never raised our daughter to…to…to…" She seems lost for words. She raises her finger and points it in Tom's face. "I should sue you for this!"

"Mother…Please!" Mary Ella stands up. She is crying so franticly, tears soak the front of her gown.

"You keep your filthy son away from my daughter!" is Pat's last warning to Tom before she drops her pointing finger of judgment.

"Please…Ms. Barton!" Principal Peters steps in, "Tempers are running high right now…it's not a good time to discuss this."

"So what are you people going to do about this?" Ms. Barton demands.

"This is a job for the school board, working with governmental services, Ms Barton. I will contact you both, once they've determined on what steps we need take. Meantime, I think the least said the better. So why don't we all go home right now? I'll contact you both the minute I hear something. There'll be no need for either of the children to report to school on Monday," Principal Peters announces.

"Why? Are they expelled?" Tom inquires.

"No, not expelled. It's just a leave of absence until we can sort all this out and come up with a plan of action."

"Oh, you people are all idiots!" Pat Barton takes her daughter's wrist and pulls. "Come on, Mary Ella, we're going home." The poor girl is still crying.

"Wait one minute," Principal Peters raises her palm up to halt them. She walks to the window and peers out down below. "Just what I feared…the News Media! There are cameras everywhere!"

"Oh, that's just great!" Ms. Barton declares.

"Don't worry; there's a way out the west side of the building where you can make it to your cars unseen." Principal Peters starts out the door, gesturing for all to follow. Ms. Barton, still holding onto her daughter, trails behind her. Before they are out the door, through her tears, the young girl looks into the young boy's face.

"Good-bye, Christopher."

"Good-bye, Mary Ella." He also is beginning to cry. He reaches out to touch her, but he's too late; she is gone. His hands grasp desperately at empty space.

***

In the parking lot, Tom Powell hurries to his car. Christopher follows close behind.

"Tom Powell," Tom announces aloud to the car. In a split second, the Voice Activation System recognizes his vocal pattern; and the driver's side door unlocks and opens. "Passenger door," Tom adds. Another door opens for Christopher.

In the car, Tom switches off all vocal response systems. He's in no mood to hear some excessively friendly electronic voice ask him if he likes the temperature inside the car or if he wants to hear his favorite music.

"Home," he states into the dash monitor; and they're on their way.

For half the ride, neither father nor son says a word. Suddenly, Tom reaches over, and takes hold of the giant sunflower in Christopher's lapel. "Take that stupid thing off!" he orders, opening the car window to hurl the flower out of the car.

The silence returns. It's obvious the more Tom thinks about it, the angrier he becomes. Finally, he speaks up.

"What were you thinking?" he demands to know. "I don't understand where you would get such a notion! I mean, are you serious about this girl?"

"I think so," Christopher says softly.

"You think so? You're willing to throw your whole life away for a…'I think so'?"

The car pulls into the garage and automatically turns off. As the garage door closes, they remain seated.

"What were you thinking?" Tom continues in disbelief, "Whatever possessed you? I mean, taking a girl…a *female* to a dance! That's sick! I'm sure you don't get that from me!"

A long moment of uncomfortable silence passes; Tom sighs long and hard.

"When we get inside, don't say anything to Doug; let me handle him. You just go to your room."

Christopher gets out of the car, Tom does too.

"This is going to kill Doug, you know? It's going to break his heart! Is that what you want, to kill your mother?" Tom demands. The boy says not a word as he enters the house with Tom following close behind.

THE END

10

1 EDEN PLACE

Everett read the address written on the slip of paper and compared it to the address engraved in the brass plate on the side of the stone wall of the front gate. They were the same, 1 Eden Place. He looked past the bars of the front gate, past the rolling hills of flowers, to the mansion on the hill. He was awestruck; he'd never seen a home so grand and luxurious. He nearly jumped out of his skin when a stern-looking security guard appeared, looking at him through the bars of the front gate.

"May I help you?" the guard asked.

"Ah, yes, I'd like to see the owner, please."

"Do you have an appointment?"

"Ah, not really, yes and no…"

"Yes and no'…?" the guard asked in a suspicious tone.

"What I mean is, I think he's expecting me. I mean, I hope he is."

The guard opened a small box attached to the wall. There was a phone; he put the receiver to his head. "Cherub here at the front gate. Sorry to bother you, sir; but there's a…" He looked to Everett for a name.

"Everett Body."

"There's a Mr. Everett Body to see you, sir. Yes, I understand. Right away, sir."

He hung up and pulled a lever. The gate opened.

The guard pointed his hand and fishtailed it as he spoke. "It's simple; you just follow the road through the garden. No need for confusion when you go through the forest, just keep to the road.

After the forest, you'll come to a clearing; and an eighth of a mile up is the mansion. The master is expecting you."

Everett followed his instructions. As he walked up the marble stairs leading to the front door of the mansion, the door opened. Out stepped a dignified, white-haired gentleman with a greeting smile.

"Good day. My name is Lord Godfrey. May I help you?"

"Yes, my name's Everett Body; just recently, after doing some research, I've learned that my great-great-grandparents once lived in this mansion."

"Really," Godfrey said. "I do remember renting it out, but that was a long time ago. What were their names?"

"Their names were Adamson, sir."

"Adamson....Adamson," Godfrey murmured as he searched memory. "Adamson! Oh, yes; now I remember. Horrible people, as I recall. They didn't pay their rent, trashed the place, and broke the lease in a thousand ways. I finally had to evict them."

"I know, and that's why I'm here. I don't see why I have to suffer for my grandparent's mistakes. I'd like to move into the mansion."

"My good man," Godfrey said. "You're not suffering *for* you grandparent's mistakes; you're suffering *because* of your grandparent's mistakes."

"I live in a small garage apartment in a terrible part of town. Please, let me move in here!"

"I'm sorry," Godfrey said. "I'm afraid there is no way. You see, I live here with my family; and I don't see how you could fit in."

"There must be someway," Everett pleaded. "I'd be willing to pay you rent every month; and I'd pay all the back rent since my grandparents' eviction."

"You don't know what you're asking," Godfrey said. "If all you can afford is a garage apartment, you couldn't afford to live here."

"I could work in the garden, do odd jobs, pay my way as I go," Everett replied.

"You couldn't work hard enough or long enough to pay even a portion of the rent," Godfrey said. "You don't understand. The rent is five million a month, and that's not counting all the back rent you'd have to pay since your grandparents' eviction. There's no way you could work off all that debt."

Just then, a handsome young man dressed in white cotton pants and shirt, holding a tennis racket came dashing up smiling.

"Good morning, Father," the young man said, smiling at Everett.

"Good morning, Jay. Jay this is Mr. Everett Body. Mr. Body, this is my son, Jay." Godfrey motioned to Everett. "Mr. Body's family used to live here. He was hoping to move in. I was just telling him how expensive it would be between the rent and the back rent; and I haven't even mentioned the first and last month's rent, as well as the nonrefundable deposit."

"That is a problem," Jay said, his face growing thoughtful. Then the smile returned as he addressed Everett. "I've got an idea. I've a sizable trust fund. Why don't I pay the bill, Father can adopt you, and you live with us rent free?"

"Adopt me?" Everett questioned.

"Yes," Jay said. "Family members don't need to pay rent. Besides, I've always wanted a younger brother. Think of it! We could play tennis everyday! Won't that be great?"

"I don't know if I like the idea," Everett said. "Can I think it over?"

"Of course you can," Godfrey said. "We'll be here, waiting."

Everett turned and followed the path he had come by. When he got to the front gate, the guard opened it for him.

"Did everything go well, sir?" Cherub asked.

"I'm not sure," Everett said. "I need to think things over. I may be back tomorrow."

"That's if there is a tomorrow," the guard murmured.

"Excuse me, what did you say?" Everett asked.

"Nothing, sir, just thinking out loud. You have a nice day, sir."

THE END

11

POLITICALLY INCONCEIVABLE

A lone penguin waddles across the marble floor to the far end of the Grand Hall where the Council of Birds awaits.

"I've come, speaking for all my comrade penguins," he announces.

"And how can we help you, Brother Bird?" the Great Bald Eagle asks, perched in the center of the line of the Birds of Council.

"We want it marked in the Great Book that we penguins are flying birds."

"I was unaware penguins have the ability to fly, what with such short wings and all," says the Quail.

"Oh yes, we do so remarkably well," the Penguin says with pride.

"May we see a demonstration?" the Flamingo asks.

"Of course," the Penguin agrees, waddling to one end of the Council then to the other, finally to center again.

"There," the Penguin proclaims, looking pleased.

"Please, forgive me, I'm not trying to offend you," the Seagull says. "You do what you do incredibly well and with such great finesse and emotion, but it's nothing I'd define as flying. You waddled."

"Then the very definition of flight must change!" the Penguin shouts. "It's unfair the Great Book will mark some birds as flying birds and others not. What we penguins do is just another form of flying; and to degrade us by calling our form of flight 'waddling' is low, cruel, and un-birdly."

"Yes, but it's still just waddling," the Great Owl interrupts. "To redefine the definition of flight will not only be wrong, but it will degrade the true meaning of flight. I'm sorry; but what you do is not flying. It's waddling."

"Is this the answer of the Council?" the Penguin asks.

"I'm afraid so," the Eagle says.

"Well, this won't be the last of it," the Penguin says as he angrily turns and waddles off.

The next few months, legions of penguins march around the Great Hall, carrying protest signs and chanting slogans of unfairness and prejudice. Rumor has it, some on the Council receive gifts from the penguins and their sympathizers. Thousands of petitions arrive daily in protest of the unfair mistreatment of all penguins.

"I don't know what to do. I find I'm pressured from all sides," the Crow says. "Can't we bend the rules slightly to include waddling as a lesser form of flight?"

"They won't have it," snaps the Dove. "It's all or nothing. They gain more sympathy with each passing day. We either give into their demands, or we are up against a fight I swear we will never win."

A long moment of silence passes till the Eagle speaks, "Very well. All those who wish to include the act of waddling as part of the defining of flight, please raise your wing."

The vote is slow and reluctant; but in the end, the new definition of flight in the Great Book includes waddling.

Weeks pass without incident, till one day a lone chicken stands before the Great Council.

"I've come speaking for all my comrade chickens," she announces.

"How can we help you, Fellow Bird?" the Great Bald Eagle asks.

"We want it marked in the Great Book that we chickens are flying birds."

All on the Council look to one another in disbelief.

"May we see a demonstration of what you call flight?" the Hawk asks.

The Chicken scratches and pecks at the ground.

"That looks more like pecking and scratching, if you ask me," the Blackbird declares.

"Perhaps it seems so from where you're perched; but to us chickens, it is flight…beautiful flight.

If you can grant that this," he waddles about in a poor imitation of a penguin, "is flight, then surely the noble and majestic gestures of us chickens you must consider as flight!"

It takes one vote; scratching and pecking are, along with waddling, now to be considered flight.

***

For the next few weeks, group after group of birds without the ability of flight stand before the Great Council demanding placement in the Great Book as birds of flight. There are representatives for the Ostriches, Emus, Cassowaries, Kiwis, Rheas, just to name a few; even a lone Dodo, a species most thought to be extinct.

The next issue brought under consideration was that birds of true flight – though they disallowed use of the term – must not degrade the efforts of the non-flying birds. The only solution was to ban all true flight. No longer would there be soaring, diving, floating, or true flight. All birds would waddle, scratch, peck, and crawl to whatever their destination is.

Of course, this doesn't sit well with the birds of true flight; but in solidarity, they do their best to comply. Nevertheless, it wasn't till early fall of that year that their judgment came back to bite them with a vengeance.

"There are millions of birds who normally fly south for the winter," says the Thresh. "Without true flight," he dares to say the phrase, "many will not escape the oncoming of the winter's bitter cold; and they will die!"

"There is no other way," the Eagle says. "In all fairness and to stay true to our word, many will die. It is sad, but we have given our word."

Just then, the entire Council looked up to see, of all things, a large brown bear standing before them.

"Yes, Brother of the Forest, how may we help you?" the Eagle asks. "Have you come to speak for others of your kind?"

"No, I come to speak just for my own."

The entire Council breathes a sigh of relief.

"So, how may we help you?" the Eagle repeats.

The Bear hesitates for a moment. "I know you see before you a large, burly, brown-haired grizzly; but inwardly, all my life I have felt a closer kinship with the birds of the air. A delicate peacock trapped in the confines of this hefty brut. I have made plans. I plan to have my body shaved, my teeth filed down, my ears clipped; and already I have shed hundreds of pounds. I only ask that after the transformation, my name will find its way into the Great Book of Birds."

Each of the Bird Council sighs, slowly and sadly. After all they had previously granted, how could they deny one more soul its heart's desire? They look at one another with the same question in their eyes: where will this all end?

THE END

12

TROUBLE AT THE PEARLY GATES

Peter sat at his desk, writing with his head down. He needn't look up to know Crenshaw was standing in the doorway.

"Yes, Crenshaw, what is it? Make it quick; I'm busy."

"I know that, sir. I am sorry, sir; but we're having some trouble at the gate. I'm afraid it's a call for upper-management."

Peter looked up, blinking. "What could be so difficult? What is it, another one of the lost souls complaining that they don't deserve to be turned away? Give them our deepest apologies and give them the map to *The Other Place*...Too bad, so sad."

"It's not like that, sir," Crenshaw said. "I really think you need to speak with this one yourself."

"Very well, send them in."

"Very good, sir. Thank you, sir." Crenshaw placed the file on the desk before leaving.

A moment later, a man entered and stood at the door. He was squatty and very mousy with dark eyes and hair, and a nose that protruded farther than most. A fair description of him would be that he was unimpressive and unmemorable. He wore the white flowing robe common to all the after-lifers; only his was equipped with the generic white waist cord, unlike Peter's gold cord.

Peter opened the folder. "Archibald Beechcroft, fifty-eight, died thirty-seven minutes ago.

Death was the result of eating some bad fish. Must have been uncomfortable; but still, there are worse ways to go. Wouldn't you agree, Mr. Beechcroft? Please, take a seat."

Peter thumbed through the papers. "Looking at your file, Mr. Beechcroft, everything seems in order. You clearly fit the entire criterion to gain entrance into Heaven. So what is the problem, Mr. Beechcroft?"

His voice was as unobtrusive as his looks. "I must say everyone's been nice since I arrived. I had a look around, and I just don't think the place is right for me. Not a good fit, so to speak."

"I don't understand, Mr. Beechcroft. This is *Heaven*, your eternal reward."

"That's just my point. I don't think I could be happy here. An eternity here would be you-know-what for me."

"I still don't understand, Mr. Beechcroft. I mean, look at what we offer. Pearly gates, streets paved with gold, mansions to live in, and dinner with the Boss every night, anything your heart desires. What is it about the place that doesn't suit you?"

"To put it in one word it's *People*. There are all these people here. I've had enough of them. I'd rather be alone."

Peter raised one finger up, making a point. "Love thy neighbor as thyself."

"Yes, I have. Just look at my file, it proves that I do. I couldn't pass the muster if I didn't love my neighbor. I did that for a lifetime. Now I want to be left alone. I loved my mother with all my heart, but eventually I had to stop living with her and move out on my own when I was thirty-eight. I never stopped loving my mother, but I was much happier living in that cheap, little apartment."

Peter rubbed his chin. "I see your point, but what do you suggest we do? We can't send you back for rebirth; we're not Hindus, you know. You don't deserve sending to *The Other Place*."

"There *are* more people there than here," Beechcroft commented.

"That's true," Peter agreed. "Tell me, Mr. Beechcroft, what is with you and people? What's so bad about people?"

"Well, I'm not one to point fingers. I'm not better than anyone else. Still, that's just the point. People are so like…" He hesitated. "…like people, if you know what I mean."

"I understand," Peter said sympathetically. "I was there too, if you remember. We can be a difficult lot." Peter shook his head and tapped his pencil on the desk. "Mr. Beechcroft, what are we to do with you?"

"Can't you just drop me on some planet and leave me?"

"I'm afraid we can't do that. Heaven is your new home, Mr. Beechcroft."

"Well, I'm sure it's a big place. Isn't there some desolate area where I could stay?"

"Yes, there is. It's just that such places are for reflection and meditation, and only used for short periods of time." He put his pencil down and smiled. "You see, Mr. Beechcroft, *Heaven* is more than a place. It's a way of being; it's about relationships, relationships with the Man upstairs and your fellow man. I'm afraid there is no alternative."

"Oh, my, my, my," Beechcroft said. "Heaven or not, it all sounds so *Hellish* to me."

"We try not to use that word, here, Mr. Beechcroft," Peter said. "However, I can see your problem." Peter jumped from his seat and walked to a large map in a frame hung on the wall. "Wait one minute. I think I have a solution. It's a big universe, Mr. Beechcroft." He pointed to a spot on the map. "There is a place in *Heaven* where souls of a particular planet stay. Far advanced they are. I think you'd get along swimmingly with them. Why don't you spend a year with them; and after that time, we'll see how you feel about staying there."

"An entire year…?" Beechcroft said in dismay.

"Mr. Beechcroft, we're looking at eternity. In the scheme of things, a year isn't even a drop in the bucket. Of course you'll remain a novitiate. You'll stay the way you are and not change until you decided where you want to spend your time without end." Peter reached across the desk and buzzed the intercom. "Crenshaw, I need you to escort Mr. Beechcroft to Section E."

"Yes, but, sir," Crenshaw replied. "Section E is for…"

"I know what Section E is for, Crenshaw. Just do as I tell you." He looked up and smiled. "Well, Mr. Beechcroft, it's been a little slice of Heaven meeting you. Crenshaw will take you where you need to go. We'll see you in a year's time. Good day, Mr. Beechcroft." He sat down again and continued where he'd left off.

***

There are no words, no sound, the human voice can utter that can describe what Section E looks like. There are some words that will point you in the right direction, such as beautiful, grand, and spacious; but these adjectives fail miserably.

To describe the souls that inhabit Section E of *Heaven* is even more useless. At first, they all look the same; but with closer inspection, you can see many subtle differences. Each is tall and slender – none are less than six feet. Their garbs are blue, white, and silver robes, all long and shiny. Beechcroft found it impossible to look any of them in eye, as each shone as bright as a sun. There is no talking in Section E, no words that is. All communication is telepathic, and it is all images. No one goes by any name, but they always address one another with love and respect. There are no days in Sections E. For time is not spent; it just is.

Still a novitiate and not yet transformed, Beechcroft was only aware of what went on in Section E; he did not share in it. These creatures worked, played, slept, ate, danced, sang, prayed, and lived for God and with God, in a way Beechcroft never knew was possible.

The more they gave, the more they received. These noble creatures existed in a realm of joy that Beechcroft could only hope one day to understand. It ate at him with the passing of time. It started as envy, turned to jealousy, and then ended in heartbreak. Beechcroft could take it no more; and when that moment came, Crenshaw appeared and brought him back to Peter's office.

"So, Mr. Beechcroft, I'm surprised to see you," Peter said. "It hasn't even been a week."

"I couldn't take it any longer," Beechcroft cried. "It was so wonderful, but I was still an outsider. I want to be with those people, I want to be like them, and live the life they live. Please, let it be so."

Peter spoke into the intercom. "Crenshaw, will you come here, please." He smiled at Beechcroft. "I'll have Crenshaw take you back. You'll no longer be novitiate; and soon you will be just like everyone else in Section E. I'm glad you found your place in Heaven, Mr. Beechcroft."

"Thank you," Beechcroft said as he walked toward Crenshaw waiting for him at the doorway. He tuned just before leaving. "Still, there's one thing," Beechcroft asked. "Those wonderful beings in Section E, where in the universe did they come from?"

"Don't you know, Mr. Beechcroft?" Peter said. "Section E...the E stands for Earthlings. You're going where we were going to send you in the first place, to be with your people, with your own kind."

"I don't understand," Beechcroft said. "They're nothing like the people I knew on earth."

Peter smiled. "Don't you remember, Mr. Beechcroft? *'Therefore, if any man be in Christ he is a new creature. Old things are passed away; behold, all things are become new!'*"

THE END

13

THE GOD WHO HAS NO NAME

Isu was just a boy; but tall and strong, he could handle responsibility better than most men twice his age. He respected and loved his father, more so over the year since the death of his mother. Many people frowned on the only son of the wealthiest man in the valley doing something as menial as shepherding. But he enjoyed and took great pride in watching over the flocks of his father. His happiest moments were when he was alone in the hills with his sheep, with the beauty of nature and the quiet peace that allowed him to think clearly.

Isu waited on the approach of his fifteenth birthday, when his father promised they would sail across the great sea to visit the palace of the pharaoh and perhaps even to glimpse the living god. He knew about the gods; he'd studied about them all his life. But to see one in the flesh would be amazing.

It was midday, and the hot sun wavered high in the sky. Isu shaded his eyes and looked back towards home. A thick, black smoke billowed up. Without a single thought of the welfare of his sheep, Isu ran toward home. When he came down from the hills, he saw his home in flames; people were running about the property in chaos. His father was walking toward him.

"Father, what is the matter?" Isu shouted.

His father did not answer. There was a tortured look on his face and fear in his eyes. When he was a few feet from Isu, he reached out for his son and fell facedown onto the ground, a spear sticking in his back. Isu rushed to him, pulled the spear out, fell to his knees, and turned his father over.

"Father, speak to me."

Isu held his father in his arms. Little life was left in the old man as he spoke in a whisper.

"Robbers, Isu. Robbers come to kill us and take everything we own. They are men sent by the magistrate. They know the law. You are my only son and heir. You are all that stands between the magistrate from taking ownership of our land. They will kill you if they catch you. You must run for you life, my son. Go! Run, Isu, run as fast and as far as you can."

"I won't leave you, father," Isu wept, but it was too late. His father died in his arms.

He heard shouting coming closer every second. Isu knew what he had to do. He gently rested his father on the ground, stood, and began to run up the hill.

At the top of the hill, he turned and looked back. At least a dozen robbers were in pursuit, their swords drawn. Under the shade of a tree, Isu fell to his knees.

"Oh great Wadjet, Sister of Nekhbet, Goddess of Protection, cover me and protect me from my enemies who seek to kill me." Isu looked down the hill; the small band was approaching fast. He stood and held his arms to the sky. "Mafdet, God of Justice, smite those who have killed my father." Nothing happened.

Isu turned and ran as fast as he could down the side of the hill, into the valley. He looked over his shoulder to see the robbers at the top of the hill, pointing down at him and then running toward him.

"Mighty Ra, Great Golden Disk in the Sky, they are so close to you. Send down your ray of sunlight to blind them." They continued down the hill. Isu cried out again, "Geb, God of the Earth, let rocks roll and crash on my pursuers, make the earth open and swallow my enemies. Deliver them into the hands of Osiris, God of the Underworld, so he may drag them down to his realm where they will weep forever." Again, the gods were silent. Isu began running.

Scrambling through the deep woods, Isu lifted up prayers to as many gods as he could remember.

Apophasis, God of Snakes and Chaos… perhaps he would send the robbers running in circles and so they would fall into a snake pit. Maybe Horus, God of the Sky and Falcons, and Nekhbet the Vulture God would send birds of prey down on them. Perhaps, Sekhmet, Goddess of Vengeance and lions, would send wild beasts after them, or Shu, God of Wind and Air, would send a gale to wipe them off the face of the earth. Still nothing, no sign from the gods; and the sound of the men shouting in the distance behind him seemed closer.

Not thinking of what direction he was going, before long, he found himself on the banks of the great river with no alternative but to forge it. He dove in, and immediately the current took hold of him. Isu swam fast and hard, but he moved faster downstream than across stream. Finally, he made it to the other side, exhausted. Taking no time to rest; he jumped up and began to run. He thought surely the robbers would give up their pursuit at the river, but he heard their shouts and splashes as they jumped into the water. He murmured a quick prayer to Sobek the God of Crocodiles and Alligators, to have them swallowed up; but he heard no screams of terror.

Isu gasped at the top of the next hill and stumbled down the other side. Miles of desert lay before him. He paused for one more prayer.

"Great god Amun, Amun Ra, King of all the Gods, the mightiest of them all, hear my prayer. Save me from the hands of my enemies, smite them; and I will build an altar to you and sacrifice a tenth of all that was once my father's and is now mine." Isu waited for a sign; but all he saw were the miles of sand before him, reflecting the hot sun that hung in the sky. He continued running.

Isu wondered how much farther he could run. The heat coming from above and mirroring off the sand was like being in an oven. He felt his skin burning, his feet and tongue swelling. His throat was so parched, it hurt to swallow.

His vision began to blur. He thought certainly the robbers would be suffering as much as he, and would give up the hunt. He looked back over his shoulder. There was a fair separation between them, but they were there.

They were now just small specks bobbing up and down in the distance but still in pursuit.

Why had the gods forsaken him? Were his prayers not right, his sacrifices too small? Had he grieved them in someway, unknowingly blasphemed or transgressed against them? Did they not see? Did they not care? Then a thought rose in him that made him tremble inside. Did they not exist?

Up ahead, Isu saw a hazy line along the horizon. As he moved on, the line became clearer. Every few minutes, as he rushed on and got closer, the line became taller. When he was less than a mile away, he knew what it was. It was a high hill of sand. As he approached it, he noticed sparse foliage on it. He reach the hilltop, sweating and out of breath.

His heart sank as he stood looking at what lay before him. More sand, but this was different...it was the shoreline. He had run all the way to the sea. As far as he could see in all directions, left, right, and forward, he saw nothing but sky and sea. He ran down to the water's edge. Large waves crashed and seemingly disappeared into the beach. The water rushed forward across his feet and then receded, eroding the shoreline; and he felt its pull trying to draw him in. There was nowhere to run or hide. He knew he had little time before the robbers would be on him. He fell to his knees, held out his arms, and shouted to the sky.

"I look around me. I look at the world, and I know there is a god. It is all so perfect; there must be a god. Everything is in perfect balance, placed there with care and intelligence. I know there is a god. I know you are there; but I don't know your name. Oh, creator of all things on earth and in heaven, help me. Oh, God who has no name, save me!"

At that moment, the water began to separate, moving away from to his right and left, farther and farther till there was a dry walk in the sea a mile wide. He was stunned but relieved for somewhere to run. He jumped to his feet, rushed down into the depths of the sea, yet stood on dry land. He ran forward as fast as he could. The walls of water on both sides were nearly as high as the width of the path he was on. He hoped the robbers would be too frightened to follow him, but he couldn't take that chance so he continued running.

After a while, Isu looked on and saw some miles ahead the path covered with stones, thousands upon thousands of stones. Focusing, he noticed something strange. These stones were moving. As he got closer, he realized they weren't stones; they were people, thousands of people. When he got close enough to make out their faces, he saw they were being lead by an old man with long white hair and beard and carrying a long walking stick. When they were a few feet apart, the old man raised his hand to halt the thousands marching behind him.

"Who are you, boy?" the old man asked.

"My name is Isu. There is a band of robbers behind me, hunting me down to kill me."

"How many are there?"

"There's at least a dozen."

The old man laughed. "Don't worry. When they see how many we are, they'll run from you." The old man took hold of the boy's shoulder and turned him around. They began walking; the others began the march, again.

"Who are you?" Isu asked as they walked on.

"My name is Moses, and these are my people. There's no need to be afraid."

"I'm no longer afraid," Isu said. "I have prayed to the one true God, the God who has no name; and he opened the sea before me."

"Did he, now?" Moses said gently. "And you don't know his name?"

"I should have asked, but I didn't," Isu said.

"I once asked," Moses said. "And do you know what he said?"

Isu shook his head.

"He said, 'I am that I am.'"

"I don't understand," Isu said, sounding confused.

"Come, I'll explain it to you as we go."

THE END

14

23 HRS & 20 MIN + 40 MIN

Clark pulled his new T-Bird up to the curb and stopped in front of the ranch-style home on Redondo Drive. He honked the horn three long times; Daniel came running out, holding his notebook under one arm and a brown paper bag in the other. Once seated in the car, Daniel placed the notebook on his lap and the bag on the front seat between them. Clark gunned the engine, put it in gear; and they sped off leaving tire marks in the street.

"So, what's this all about; why the hubbub?" Daniel asked trying not to slide in his seat as Clark took the turns at high-speed.

"Murphy is fit to be tied. They found something, so it's all hands on deck."

"What did they find?" Daniel asked.

"You got me. It was either too hard to explain on the phone or too top secret. You do know they've tapped the phones, don't you?"

Daniel only nodded.

Clark glanced at the bag between them. "What'cha got there?"

"My lunch," Daniel replied.

"You do know we have a cafeteria at work, and we get to eat free?"

Daniel laughed. "You couldn't get me to eat all those chemicals, if you paid me."

Clark quickly peered again into the bag. "What is this? Danny, is that your Bible? What are ya bringing your Bible to work for? You know it makes Murphy mad as a wet hen."

"It's 1969," Daniel said. "As far as I know, it's still a free country. I have the right to practice my religion how I see fit."

"Danny, do you want to stay on Murphy's bad side? He may not have the right to fire you, but there's nothing that says he can't make your life miserable."

"I'm willing to risk it," Daniel said.

Clark continued. "Besides, we're both scientists, we have the word 'Doctor' before our names and several letters on the end. We're paid large sums of money to make discoveries in this century, not to decipher myths written by primitives thousands of years ago."

Daniel took the Bible in one hand and shook it. "There's nothing in this book that doesn't line up with scientific thought."

"Yeah, sure," Clark said sarcastically.

Daniel placed the Bible back in the bag. "Go ahead and laugh. Most of us have at one time or another, including myself. Only, one day you're gonna want to know more about the Bible; and on that day you know what I'm gonna do?"

"No, what's that?"

"I'm gonna bite my tongue from saying 'I told ya so' and tell you everything I can."

Just then, they pulled up and stopped at the front gate; a soldier stepped out of the guardhouse and bent low, looking into the car. The two scientists displayed their photo IDs.

"Who's here?" Clark asked the sergeant.

"Everybody," the soldier replied. "All the big brains are here. It must be something big."

"Do you know what?" Daniel asked.

"You guys are the ones running the show. I'm just the guy watching the front door. You tell me."

"Thanks," Clark said.

"Good luck," shouted the sergeant as they drove forward.

They parked next to Lieberman who was sitting in his car going over his notes. They all got out of their cars and smiled at one another.

'So what's this all about?" Clark asked Lieberman.

"Search me," Lieberman said. "I got a call from Murphy first thing this morning. He was beside himself."

"Well, I guess the only way to find out is to head on in," Clark surmised.

Murphy stood at the head of the long conference table in the meeting room. Seated on both sides of the table were some of the greatest minds of the time.

"We're somewhere between a rock and a hard place," Murphy announced. "As you know, we've done some computer programs to predict where the planets and the stars will be in the future. This has been worthwhile. If we are to launch a probe, we know where it will be in a year or more. Lately, we've looked in the other directions. Where were the planets and the stars in the past? We could pinpoint any heavenly body's position back for thousands of years. Only recently, we've discovered there is an entire day missing somewhere in the past. An entire twenty-four hours we cannot account for. I want everyone working on this till we find that missing day."

"Have you double-checked the data?" Doctor Matsumoto asked.

"No, not double-checked. We must have looked at the data a hundred times; and it always comes up 24 hours short," Murphy replied. "We've checked the equipment, as well. There just isn't a simple answer for this."

Daniel raised his hand.

Murphy acknowledged Daniel. "Doctor Wade, you have an idea?"

"Begging you pardon, sir; but I do think there is a simple answer for this. It's all here in Bible." He said this as he reached under the table and came up holding his Bible.

"Oh, not that again," Doctor Fenstermacher said laughing. "Give us a break from your fantasy book, will you, Wade?"

"They're not fantasies!" Daniel insisted.

Doctor Fenstermacher shook his hand in the air, smirking. "Oh, like your theory the earth is only six-to-ten thousand years old." Mostly everyone at the table laughed. "The entire universe created in six days. We're scientists here, Wade, not children who believe there's a man with a great, white beard who lives in the sky." There was more laughter.

"Stop it! Stop it!" Doctor Biobaku shouted. He stood up, his arms straight and his fists resting on the table. He stared down each person until the laughter stopped. "You say you're scientists! Well, then starting acting like scientists!"

"Are you saying you believe in the Bible, also, Doctor?" Doctor Kozlov asked with a smirk on her lips.

"I'm saying a true scientist never mocks a colleague." He pointed at Daniel. "This man says he has a theory. I don't care where it comes from. I will not believe or disbelieve in it until I've run it through the scientific process. If we close our minds and only consider what we think to be true, humanity will come to standstill."

"We'd be wasting our time," Doctor Fenstermacher said, pounding his fist on the table. "That book is nothing but folklore and myths."

"Have you ever studied folklore and myths, Doctor?" Doctor Biobaku asked as he calmly sat down. "You'll find that most of them are based in truth. I say it's our only lead, and we should investigate."

"With whose time and money will you do this?" Doctor Kozlov asked.

Daniel placed the Bible in the center of the table and looked into their eyes. "What are you so afraid of?"

There was a long silence. Murphy stood up. "Very well. Doctor Wade, tell us your theory."

Daniel took up the Bible and thumbed through the pages. "It's in the book of Joshua, Joshua 10:13 to be exact. He was the leader of the Hebrews as they entered Canaan. Actually, he was more of a general, since they fought so many wars with the surrounding peoples."

"I should have known it would have to do with violence," Doctor Fenstermacher murmured.

Daniel ignored the remark and continued. "The Israelites were fighting the Amorites. On the field of battle, with the help of the Lord, the Israelites were winning; but time was running short. Joshua asked for God's help." Daniel began to read from his Bible. "So the sun stood still, and the moon stopped, till the nation avenged itself on its enemies."

"You see, that proves it's the writing of uneducated idiots," Doctor Kozlov claimed. "Every civilized person knows the sun cannot stop in the sky, because the sun doesn't move. The sun remains stagnate; it is the earth that moves."

Daniel smiled at her. "Doctor Kozlov, tell me, have you ever seen a beautiful sunrise or sunset?"

"Of course I have," she declared.

"How is that possible?" Daniel asked. "The sun isn't moving. It can't rise or set. It just appears to do so. Therefore, we express it in these terms. It's a figure of speech, a way of describing what all of us experience."

Again, there was a long silence.

"Alright, everyone listen up," Murphy announced. "As Doctor Biobaku pointed out, this is our only lead, so let's go for it. Doctor Kozlov, you will be head of the investigation. The next meeting will be when we've finish. Thank you, that is all."

***

Three weeks later, Doctor Kozlov announced the study complete. Every one of the scientist gathered once more around the conference table. Immediately, Murphy noticed there was one too many heads seated at the table. A stranger sat next to Daniel. Murphy addressed the problem.

"Doctor Wade, who is this man sitting next to you."

"I beg your patience," said Daniel. "He is here at my invite with information that I'm sure will be enlightening. First, let us hear the findings of the study."

"Very well," Murphy said. He turned to Doctor Kozlov. "Well, Doctor, what are your findings?"

She looked across at Daniel. There was a pompous tone to her voice. "We ran many computer programs on the said information. We checked the data and rechecked it. There is no doubt.

As I originally suspected, this whole Joshua theory comes up short. As you know, we are looking for a missing 24 hours. After careful study, this so-called stopping of the sun in the Bible comes up short.

Our findings show that it could only have been 23 hours and 20 minutes, 40 minutes short of a full day." She directed her next words to Daniel. "I'm afraid, Doctor, after thorough, scientific investigation, your theory proves to be what we suspect, a myth and nothing more."

"That is a shame," Murphy said with a touch of sarcasm.

Daniel raised his hand. "Sir, I would like to introduce the expert I've invited here today." He turned to the stranger. "This is Wayne Braddock, the pastor of my church."

Doctor Fenstermacher pointed a finger at Daniel. "Doctor, you do understand this is a scientific investigation, and not the Spanish Inquisition?"

"If you'd just hear him out, I think we can come to a conclusion," Daniel said.

Pastor Braddock stood, opened his Bible and addressed the gathering. "I praise you for finding the missing 23 hours and 20 minutes. That is a great achievement. Now, you say there is still 40 minutes unaccounted for. Let us turn to second Kings 20:9-11. Hezekiah, the Israeli leader at the time, asked for a sign from God. The sign was that the Lord made the shadow on the stairway of Ahaz go back ten steps. The sun receded. If you do the math, you will find that it is the missing 40 minutes."

After a long silence, Murphy spoke. "Well, let's look at this additional information and see what we find." He directed this to Doctor Kozlov.

***

Clark found Daniel seated behind his desk in his home office.

"I heard you got canned. I'm sorry. What happened?"

Daniel looked up at Clark and smiled. "They ran the program. It seems I was right. Hezekiah's story about turning back of the sun for ten steps did account for the missing 40 minutes. When Murphy called me to his office, I thought for a moment I would receive praise and honor. Instead, I got a pink slip and a clear explanation why the findings would never go public."

A solemn look washed over Clark's face. "Danny, I'd like you to do me a favor. I don't care if you do say 'I told you so'; I'd like to hear more about this Bible of yours."

THE END

15

THE THIEF ON THE RIGHT

After swallowing the last bite of his hamburger, Billy washed it down with the last swig of his vanilla milk shake.

"Was everything to your liking?" Warden Jefferies asked, looking through the bars of Billie's cell.

Billy held up the last of his French fries and waved it in the air. "Give my compliments to the chef, warden."

"Good. That's what we like to hear. We pride ourselves in giving a man a good last meal."

"It was as good as the burgers at the Dairy Queen," Billy said, "maybe better."

"Good, good," Warden Jefferies said. "There is one last thing, Billy. I hate to bring it up, but there's only six more hours till midnight. Would you like to talk to a preacher?"

Billy laughed. "You want me to spend my last few hours gettin' ear-bangin' from some *Holy Joe*?"

"It might be good for you, Billy."

"What do you know about what's good for me? I know a lot of better ways to spend my last few hours than with a Holy Joe." Suddenly, Billy jumped up and tossed the food tray against the cell wall. "I'll tell you what, warden. You send in that Holy Joe. I'd like to give him a piece of my mind. In fact, I'd like to spit in his eye, since I can't spit in God's."

"You shouldn't talk like that, Billy."

"Why not? It's all a fairytale, ain't it? Besides, what you gonna to do…kill me?" He laughed even louder.

Warden Jefferies turned and walked away. He was met by Reverend Clyde Turner, pastor of the Shepherd's Flock Baptist Church, just six miles from the prison.

"So what did he say?" Reverend Turner asked.

"He'll see you; but I tell you, Clyde, he ain't gonna be none too friendly."

"That's alright," Turner said. "If it were easy, everybody'd be doin' it."

The Reverend walked up to Billy's cell and took hold of the bars. "Warden Jefferies says you'd be willin' to speak with me."

"Are you the Holy Joe around here?" Billy asked.

"The name's Clyde, and I certainly ain't holy. I am an ordained minister, if that's what you mean. Warden Jefferies said you'd like to talk."

"Did he tell you I wanted to spit in your eye?"

"No, but he hinted you weren't keen on religion. You mind if I come in?"

"It's a free country."

Clyde looked down the hall to the guard post. "Open up number nine." An alarm buzzer sounded, and the cell opened. Clyde stepped in, and the bars closed behind him. He pulled up a stool and sat down to face Billy seated on his bed.

Clyde asked point-blank. "So, what's your beef with God, Billy?"

"You know, I've seen your type all my life: passing judgment on poor folk like me, tellin' them they're gonna burn in hell."

"You think I'm passing judgment on you?"

"That's the way I see it."

"I'm just preachin' the Gospel. If you repent and trust in Jesus, you don't have to go to hell."

"What if I said that I don't believe in hell, and I think you're delusional?"

"I can understand that," Clyde said. "Only you got fewer than six hours to live. Do you feel confident enough to take that risk?"

Billy remained silent as Clyde continued.

"It's never too late, Billy. Did you know when Jesus was crucified, he had two criminals crucified with him, one to his right and one to his left? One of the criminals cursed Jesus, but the other one begged for forgiveness.

He is the only one in the Bible who received a guarantee he'd go to heaven. Jesus said, 'Truly I tell you, today you will be with me in paradise.' Only a criminal received that guarantee. You can have the same, if you just ask."

"What side of the cross was he on? That forgiven criminal, what side was he on?" Billy asked.

"I don't know," Clyde said. "I guess on the right. Do you want to be on the right side of Jesus?"

"You know, I still owe you a spit in the face, preacher; but I don't want to waste my time or my spit."

"You walk that last mile in just a few more hours, Billy. Do you mind if I walk them with you?"

"Not at all. I'll show you how a real man dies," Billy replied.

***

Clyde spent the next few hours in his office on his knees.

"Lord, let Billy's eyes open in these last few minutes. Let the Holy Sprit guide him. Somehow, I think under all that pain is a good kid. It would be a shame if heaven didn't have him as a resident. Thy will be done."

***

A few minutes before the time for the execution, a small group escorted Billy from his cell and down the hall. Two guards walked a few feet at his left and his right; one guard walked behind and one up front. The warden walked ahead of them all, and Clyde walked at his close right.

Billy whispered to Clyde, "You think I'm gonna break down at the last minute, don't you?"

"The thief at Jesus' right gained eternal reward in the last few minutes of his life, why not you? All you need do is repent of your sins and trust in Jesus."

"Forget it, preacher. I killed a man while robbing a grocery store. I'm only here because I was too slow and too stupid. That man's life meant nothing to me."

"All life is sacred and means something to God."

"Well, not to me," Billy replied.

As they passed the cells of the other prisoners on death row, they cheered him on.

"That-a boy, Billy, don't give them the satisfaction; spit in their eyes up to the last," one inmate said. "Show 'em what you're made of, boy," another said. "Keep your chin up, Billy. Laugh in their faces." "Give 'em hell, Billy." "See ya on the other side, brother."

Suddenly, Billy stopped walking. The warden stopped and turned to him.

"Keep movin', Billy."

"Where's that sound comin' from?" Billy asked.

"What sound?"

"That bell," Billy replied. "I hear a little bell, ringing and ringing."

In a flash, everything disappeared. The bell over the door was ringing. It was the door of the grocery store that Billy had robbed three years earlier where he shot and killed the owner and proprietor, Phillip Lin, a second generation Chinese immigrant.

Everything was the way Billy remembered it; only the perspective was wrong. Billy stood behind the counter watching himself enter the store. He looked in the reflective plate on the cash register. It wasn't his face; it was the face of Phillip Lin. The incident was being reenacted, but now *he* was the victim.

"May I help you?" asked Billy as Phillip Lin. In his mind, he knew what was going to happen; but he couldn't stop it; he had to continue.

The Billy before him pulled out a gun and pointed it at him. "I want all the cash."

Billy as Phillip Lin quickly fumbled through the cash register and handed over all the money.

"Fifteen stinking dollars!" shouted the Billy standing before him. "That's it, Charlie Chan; you're a dead man."

"You don't want to do that, son," said Billy as Phillip Lin.

"I ain't your son! Sayonara!" said the Billy standing before him as he pulled the trigger.

The thoughts of Phillip Lin mingled with his own. He knew the last thoughts of the man.

At the sound of the gun blast, Billy reappeared in prison. They were just entering the arena of execution. Billy turned to Reverend Clyde.

"I was wrong! The poor man I killed...all he could think of when I shot him was how his family would survive. He loved them, and he loved life. What I did was so wrong!"

"Keep moving, Billy," the warden said.

They continued walking to the front of the room where Old Sparky, the electric chair, waited. They walked past rows of seated state dignitaries and news media. Phillip Lin's family had declined the right to be present.

Suddenly, Billy heard the sound of people crying. He looked around, but there was no one in the room crying. Then the sound of thunder and rain filled his ears.

In a flash, everything disappeared. Billy found himself in the strangest of places and in the strangest of positions. He was in the desert, and he was tied to a cross. He looked down to see Roman soldiers holding spears and keeping a crowd in order. The crowd was in chaos; some were in tears. None of them were looking at him. He followed their gaze, and turned his head to see another man on a cross next to him. Only this man wasn't tied to his cross; he was nailed to it. There was so much blood. The man turned to look at him. In an instant, Billy knew who was looking at him. He held no question in his mind.

"Lord, forgive me, a sinner," Billy said. "Remember me when you come into your kingdom."

Jesus looked at him and said, "Truly I say to you, today you will be with me in paradise."

Billy became aware of the intense pain in his body. Just when he felt he would pass out, he found himself standing before Old Sparky. He turned to Clyde standing behind him.

"It's okay, Clyde. I've made my peace with the Lord. I thank you.

"Any last things you'd like to say?" the warden asked.

Billy looked at all those in the room. "I'm sorry for what I did. It was wrong. I've asked the Lord to forgive me; and he has, just like he promised. I'm finally free, and I know it. If any of you here think you're going to get away with anything, you're not. Only Jesus can set you free. And today, I am free!"

Without coxing, Billy jumped in the electric chair.

"Okay, boys, I'm ready. Come on and send me home."

THE END

16

AMAZING SIN-O-METER

Gilbert Bohack waited with great excitement every year for the week of the State Fair. Forget any other time of the year, even holidays; only two dates were circled on his calendar: his mother's birthday and the first week in October. He'd schedule one of his two vacation weeks from his job at *Downe and Spiral Accounting Firm* to spend at the State Fair.

Opening day of the fair, Gilbert was first in line, just after the parade and marching band. He held a map of the fairgrounds; on the back he'd written out a schedule for the entire week. He would not miss one exhibition, contest, or show. Between all the festivities and hoopla, there was food. He purposely lost some weight the month before in preparation for eating the highest caloric meals of the year.

He spent the first day on the midway, riding all the rides and playing all the games. Day two he explored the agricultural building. The morning of day three he dedicated to seeing the sights in the Hall of Science, and so it went throughout the week. Sunday, the last day of the fair, he spent in the Hall of Commerce.

The Hall of Commerce was row after row of small-time peddlers selling their goods. Salespeople tossed dirt on carpets and then vacuumed them clean. Others made fruit and vegetable drinks in juicers and then handed out samples in small paper cups. Gilbert sampled crackers covered with dip made in a blender that diced, sliced, puréed, pulverized, cracked, and crushed. He watched a woman, using only one hand, cut a slice of tomato so thin you could see through it, all done with a knife that would never rust or need sharpening.

In the center of the hall was a small stage. On it was a table, and above that was a large sign that read "*THE AMAZING SIN-O-METER*". Suddenly, a fanfare played out of two small stereo speakers…one on each edge of the stage. A man with a constant smile on his face held a microphone and hopped onto the stage.

"Gather around, folks; gather around. Witness the most unique product of our generation, the greatest discovery since sliced bread. It's what humanity has been waiting for since Adam and Eve. Hurry! Hurry!"

He kept repeating this like a sideshow barker till he had a large crowd standing before the stage.

"Move in close, folks. You don't wanna miss this."

Gilbert worked his way to the front. The crowd went silent.

"Life is a mystery," the announcer proclaimed. "It's filled with the unexpected and no guarantees. The only thing you can be sure of is Death and Taxes; and there ain't no product on the market that can prevent taxes."

A chuckle raced through the crowd, and their faces beamed with smiling acknowledgment.

"The bad thing about death is you're never sure which way you're gonna go: up to that great reward in the sky with clouds and harps or down below with pitchforks and fiery brimstone. One thing we do know is Good People go up and Bad People go down. So how you supposed to know if you're good enough?"

He reached across the table and held up what looked like a men's belt.

"Introducing the amazing Sin-O-Meter. It looks like an ordinary belt, but it's not. While wearing the Sin-O-Meter, you will always be aware of how much sin is contained in you, by a gentle pressure around your waist. Whenever you do some good works, you make up for your sinfulness; and the pressure eases up. As you lead a better life, feel those ugly sins simply melt away, till you are worthy of eternal reward. The Sin-O-Meter takes all the guesswork out of the afterlife."

He picked up some other belts off the table.

"The Sin-O-Meter comes in two colors: black or brown. There's a slimmer model for you ladies. And for you Hindus, we have the Karma Counter embroidered with ancient Sanskrit. That's right, everlasting peace of mind all for the low, low price of only six dollars and sixty-six cents. But wait there's more! Everyone who buys a Sin-O-Meter today will also get this."

He held up a large box with red, white, and black stripes.

"With your purchase of the amazing Sin-O-Meter, you'll receive Lou Ann's Homemade Licorice Kit. That's right, now you can make your favorite red or black licorice right in your own home. Now, who'll be the first to take advantage of this amazing offer?"

Gilbert was the first to raise his hand.

***

Back home, Gilbert read the instructions that came with his Sin-O-Meter. It was simple to use: just put it on like any other belt. The belt would tighten around you indicating the degree of sin you held. If you commit a sin, the belt tightens (a good deterrent). Whenever you do an act of good works, it counteracts the sin within you. With less sin, the belt releases pressure. The idea is to do more good works than sinning. Once your good works outweigh your sins, the Sin-o-Meter fits loose; and you're worthy of an eternity in Heaven. It made all the sense in the world to Gilbert. He felt tempted to try it on but decided to start fresh in the morning. He opened the Lou Ann's Homemade Licorice Kit and thought about going into the kitchen and whip up a batch of red licorice twits. But it was getting late, and his week vacation was at an end. He needed to get some sleep. Tomorrow it was back to work.

***

Gilbert woke with great enthusiasm. He woofed down his breakfast, washed and shaved, and then dressed for the day. Lastly, slowly and methodically, like a matador putting on his sword, he put on the Sin-O-Meter. Instantaneously, it tightened around him to a snug fit.

When he left his apartment and headed for the bus stop, he became aware that it was growing tighter.

When he got to the bus stop, it was so tight he wasn't sure he could take an entire of day of wearing it. He could hardly breathe. Still, he thought this was a good thing. It only meant he was retaining far too much sin, and needed to do some acts of goodwill to relieve the tension.

Entering the office building, Gilbert went to the newsstand.

"How was the State Fair, Gilbert?" One-Eyed Sammy, the proprietor, asked.

"Gets better every year, Sammy. The morning paper, please."

Sammy handed Gilbert the newspaper, Gilbert handed Sammy a dollar bill, and Sammy gave him his change. Walking to the elevator, Gilbert went to put the change in his pocket only to realize he held four singles and a quarter. Sammy must have mistaken Gilbert's dollar for a five-dollar bill and gave him too much. He mentally chalked this up as his good luck and Sammy's misfortune. But with each step toward the elevator, the Sin-O-Meter tightened around him till he thought he'd pass out. It was then it dawned on him that what he was doing was sinful. How could he do such a cruel thing to One-Eyed Sammy?

He turned around and headed for the newsstand. With each step, the Sin-O-Meter loosened its grip; and when he returned Sammy his change, he was back to where he started.

"There goes an honest man," One-Eyed Sammy shouted.

Gilbert felt good about himself.

***

Sitting at his desk in his cubical, Gilbert was determined to be good and to do nothing but good. He'd make up for all the things he'd done wrong; melt away all that ugly sin till finally the Sin-O-Meter was a perfect fit.

Ah, but there's the rub. The best laid plans of mice and men (and Gilbert) often go down the toilet. He bit his tongue not to say what he truly felt when he spoke with rude clients on the phone. Nearly every one of his coworkers got on his nerves with their gossip and nosiness.

His boss with his impossible demands and crude, vulgar shouting irked him. And let's not mention what went through Gilbert's head whenever Mary

Jo Kowalski walked by wearing that soft, tight, pink sweater. By eleven o'clock, Gilbert was filled with anger, hatred, jealousy, envy, gluttony, sloth, and lust. The Sin-O-Meter dug so deep into him he could hardly sit up straight; the pain was great. He needed relief, and fast. He felt he needed to do some good, somewhere, for someone; or he was sure he'd die.

At lunchtime, racked with pain, Gilbert rushed to the People's Mission Soup Kitchen around the block. He ran up to the people serving behind the line.

"I need to speak with the manager," Gilbert demanded, holding his sides.

"I'm the manager. How can I help you?" a smiling elderly woman said.

"I need to help serve lunch! Please, let me help!"

Thinking it all rather strange, but not wanting to look a gift-horse in the mouth, she handed him an apron. "Here, put this on and get to the end of the line and start dishing it out."

Gilbert worked hard and frantic till sweat poured into his eyes. If his good works were removing his sins, he certainly didn't feel it. The Sin-O-Meter burrowed into his sides. He tried more than once to take it off, but it wouldn't come loose. When lunch service was over, Gilbert didn't feel any better. He tore off his apron and ran out into the street. Franticly, he looked up and down the street till he saw what he was hoping to see. There on the corner was a panhandler holding a sign: Homeless – please help – God bless you. Gilbert ran to him, took out his wallet, and empted its contents into the man's hands.

"Say, mister, you sure you want to do this?" the panhandler said, holding the cash in both hands. "There's nearly fifty dollars here."

"I still don't feel good," Gilbert murmured as he took off his watch and handed it to the man.

"Listen, pal, are you alright?" the panhandler asked.

"It's not working! Here, take this!" Gilbert said, handing over his college ring.

The tramp handed it back. "Hey, pal, have a little school pride. You know what you need? You need a doctor or something."

"A doctor! Yeah, that's right…a doctor," Gilbert said as he ran down the street towards the city hospital.

In the emergency room, the staff used every knife and saw at their disposal but couldn't cut the belt off Gilbert.

"I'm sorry, sir," the doctor said. "I've never seen anything like this. I can't get it off you. Maybe what you need is …"

Before the doctor could finish his sentence, Gilbert was out the door and running down the street. Then he saw it: a church. Sure, it made all the sense in the world. Sin, church, religion… he knew there was some connection.

Entering the church, Gilbert looked around. The only person around was an old man mopping the floor.

"I need to speak to somebody," Gilbert said, running up.

"I'm somebody," the old man said.

"I mean, someone in authority."

"That's me. I'm the pastor here."

"You are?" Gilbert said, sounding surprised.

"The name's Gus. What's yours?"

"Listen, I need help."

"I can't help anybody, if I don't know their name. Let's start again. The name's Gus. What's yours?"

"Gilbert, my name's Gilbert."

"So what seems to be the problem, Gilbert?"

"Sin! I'm full of sin!"

"That's a fairly common complaint around here; but you came to the right place, Gilbert."

"I'm full of sin and need some church, some religion to help me get rid of it."

Just then, Gilbert noticed Gus' belt. It was a Sin-O-Meter.

"That belt! Where did you get that belt?" Gilbert shouted, pointing at Gus's belt.

"Oh, this thing? Just something I found sitting in the back of the church. Funny, one day I was in my office. I heard someone in the church shout,

'Hallelujah!' When I came to investigate, all I found was this belt. It's kind of snazzy, don't you think?"

"Doesn't it hurt you to wear it?" Gilbert asked.

"No, it fits just fine."

"Then you must be sinless," Gilbert said, in admiration.

Gus burst out laughing. "Are you kidding? I sin all the time. I try not to, but you know…" Gus picked up one of the Bibles from the front pew. "Sit down, Gilbert, and let me explain. All that talk about religion is a lot of hooey. The only thing that can take away your sin is God's grace; and that comes in the form of his son, Jesus Christ. Here, I'll show you."

For the next hour, Gus read verses from the Bible about redemption as Gilbert listened intently.

"Well, Gilbert, that's all there is to it. Repent of your sins and accept Jesus Christ as your Lord and Savior."

"That's all I have to do?"

"For salvation, yes. There's a lot more you need to do to grow as a Christian. But as for salvation, that's it."

Gilbert looked up as if he were seeing the sky through the ceiling.

"Gilbert here, God. I'm just an ordinary guy and a sinner. I don't like to be, and I don't want to be, but I am. And I'm sorry. With your help, I'll try never to sin again. I thank you for your grace and accept your son, Jesus Christ, as my Lord and Savior." Gilbert looked at Gus. "How was that?"

Gus placed his hand on Gilbert's shoulder. "I couldn't have done better myself."

In that instant, the Sin-O-Meter around Gilbert's waist began to loosen. Finally, he was able to take it off.

"Here, you keep it," Gilbert said, handing the belt to Gus.

"You sure you don't want it?" Gus asked.

"Nah, I'd rather you take it."

"Fine by me," Gus said. "Now I've got a black one *and* a brown one. I think they're kind of snazzy, don't you think?"

"So, now what do I do?" Gilbert asked.

"Well, Gilbert, first we get you a Bible." Gus handed the Bible in his hand to Gilbert. "Now that's done. Then we sign you up for the Men's Bible Study here at the church. And then I hope we see you this Sunday for service. But meanwhile, I'd hate to see you just go off on your own tonight. Why don't we find a nice restaurant and have dinner together?"

"Why spend money? I live only walking distance from here. Why don't we go to my place and have dinner?"

"That's fine," Gus said. "Just let me lock up, and we'll go." The two men stood up. "So, Gilbert, what's for dinner?"

Gilbert smiled. "Do you like licorice?"

THE END

17

THE BOOK OF ROIVAS

A flying saucer soared across the sky above New York City. It looked just like one of those flying saucers in a B movie, only without the strings attached. Most people who saw it thought it was an advertisement or a publicity stunt. No one took it seriously, but the military did. No fewer than a dozen jet planes followed close behind it. The air force sent out radio transmissions at every possible frequency, but there was no answer. Finally, the saucer gently landed on the surface of the East River, facing the United Nations Building. In no time, the navy had every available boat surrounding the saucer with all guns pointing at it. A group of Navy Seals dressed in scuba gear boarded the saucer. Immediately, a circular hatch on the ship opened. Four of the Navy Seals entered.

Inside, they found walls of unfamiliar meters, buttons, and dials. There were three glass coffin-shaped capsules, each held a sleeping man. They looked like ordinary earth men with light skin and dark hair, though they were taller and heftier than most average earth men. They wore black robes and black scarves on their heads, held in place by a large gold brooch with strange writings engraved on them. One of the aliens held a large gold-leaf book in his arms.

"Suspended animation..." one of the seals whispered.

Another spoke into a thin microphone in front of his mouth attached to an earpiece. "Rambo One, this is Captain Marana. We are in the space ship. I repeat, we are in the space ship. There are three aliens in suspended animation. We are waiting further orders."

"Captain Marana, this is Rambo One. Stand down. Keep them under armed guard on the ship. Let us know when they wake."

An hour later, the glass capsules opened; and the aliens began to stir. They began to breathe normally, their eyes opened, and they sat up.

"Stay where you are and don't move," Captain Marana ordered.

"We mean you no harm, Captain," the one holding the book said. "We'll do whatever you say."

"They speak English," one of the seal said.

"That's right," said the book holder. "We've studied your speech and customs for many years to make this journey. Please forgive me. I know this sounds cliché and perhaps comical, but I must say it. Take me to your leader."

***

Within the hour, the three strangers were sitting at a long table in a small conference room on the top floor of the UN. Seated across the table from them were three UN officials.

"My name is Baha Undeen from the country of India. These are my colleagues, Otto Goetzman from Germany; and this is Susan Deering from the United States." He hesitated. "I don't know where to start."

"Please allow me," the book holder said. "I'm sure you have a million questions. Perhaps I can answer some of them. My name is Feileb." He pointed to the other two seated on his right and left. "This is Epoh, and this is Trofmoc. We come from the planet Esimorp in the constellation that you call Centaurus. Esimorp is very similar to earth; and we, as you can see, are similar to you earthlings. Still, there are many differences, mostly in our cultures. Of course, we speak a different language. We three have studied you to prepare us for this mission. In fact, we have been watching you from afar for a long time, which is the reason we are here."

"You obviously come in peace, or your people would have sent more than three," Susan Deering said, smiling. "Are you ambassadors?"

"In a sense," Feileb said. "But a better description would be…" He looked to his comrades for the correct word.

"Missionaries," Epoh exclaimed.

"Yes, that is the word," Feileb said, smiling. "We are missionaries. You see, after examining your planet for so long, we see that you are on the path to destruction; and we've come to help."

"And how do you propose to do this?" Baha Undeen asked.

Feileb continued. "For instance, our planet has only one government and one ruler; whereas you have divided your world into many..." He looked to Trofmoc for support.

"Countries," Trofmoc added.

"That's the word, countries. We on Esimorp see this as a foolish way to be. But that is your way, and you have that right. We are not here to interfere. What does concern us is the fact there are many religions on earth. Such things can only lead to chaos, distrust, bickering, or worse. On Esimorp we have only one religion and only one God. Therefore all of our people live united in peace. That is why we've come as missionaries to share our religion and God so you *too* can live in peace."

"These people of different religions here on earth won't accept each other's religion and god. Why should they accept yours?" Otto Goetzman inquired.

"Because our God *is* the one true God," Feileb replied with confidence.

Otto Goetzman sounded annoyed. "That's what they all say. They all believe their god is the one true god. Then there are many, myself included, who don't believe in such nonsense."

"It's not nonsense," Feileb insisted. "Our God is the one true God; and if you convert, you can have the peace that we have. If you don't, I foresee nothing but sorrow for your entire planet."

Baha Undeen realized the discussion was becoming heated. Like a true diplomat, he intervened. "Let's all calm down and take this slowly. Feileb, tell us about your God."

Feileb became thoughtful. "Well, he came to our planet many years ago. He stayed with us for a just a short time. In fact, he stayed long enough to give only one sermon..."

"One sermon," Susan Deering interrupted. "That's hardly enough to base an entire world's religion on."

"Why not?" Feileb replied defensively. "It was a perfect sermon. It covered all the aspects of life. We've lived by it since, and now life is good. It can be good for you also." He took the book he held so closely, placed it on the table and slid it toward Baha Undeen. "Here, this is *The Book of Roivas*. It contains everything we know of him, everything he said and did for the short time he was with us. For many years, our linguistic specialists worked to translate it into your English language. It is all we have to offer, but it is the best we have to offer."

Baha Undeen took the book in both hands, "We thank you. Perhaps if we set up some meetings with the heads of the world's religions, you could explain this to them?"

Feileb smiled and shook his head. "That would be wonderful, but I'm afraid impossible. We have less than an hour of your time to return to our ship and sail for home. The planets and stars are aligned just right now. If we don't leave within the hour, we may never return to Esimorp."

"I understand," Baha Undeen said. "I'll have our military return you to your ship immediately."

"Hold on one minute," Otto Goetzman broke in. "We've stumbled on the most exciting news in the history of the world. Three aliens from another planet, obviously with more technology than we ever dreamed of; and you want to just let them go."

"I'm afraid I must agree," Susan Deering said. "This is far too big to let them leave."

"But we have no right to keep them here," argued Baha Undeen. He pressed a buzzer at his right hand, the door opened, and four armed guards entered. "See these men safely back to their ship," he ordered.

"Stop!" Otto Goetzman shouted as he stood up. "You have no right!"

"I have all the right," Baha Undeen answered. "I'm the senior official, and I say we let them go."

Before anyone could stop him, Otto Goetzman lifted the flap on a guard's gun holster, took out the gun, and pointed at Baha Undeen.

"I say they stay. Did you see their ship? Do you know how far they came? We could study them and their ship. That kind of power is the gift of a lifetime, and you want to let it get away," Otto Goetzman said, his nervous hand shaking the gun.

"We've already offered you the gift of a lifetime; it's all here in this book," Feileb said, taking hold of the book and standing. He slowly moved toward Otto Goetzman. "It's just one sermon. If you read it, you'll understand."

"Stand back!" shouted Goetzman, now pointing the gun at Feileb. "I'm not afraid to use this."

"Otto, there's got to be another way," Susan cautioned.

"You don't want to do this," Feileb said softly, still moving forward.

"I'll kill you, I swear."

"If you kill me, these men will stop you; and my comrades will be able go home."

"But you'll be dead," Otto warned.

"True, but I'll be with Roivas and in a better place."

Otto fired two shots into Feileb. Immediately, the guards rushed Otto, took the gun from him, and wrestled him to the floor. Feileb fell to the floor, still holding the Book of Roivas.

Baha Undeen ran to his side and fell to his knees. "Quick, call medical!" he ordered Susan.

Feileb looked up at Baha. "Please, I beg you; let my friends return to the ship and leave, before it's too late." He looked up at Epoh and Trofmoc. "Go, my friends; you know what to do."

"Take these men back to their ship. That's an order," Baha told the guards.

Without question Epoh and Trofmoc followed the guards out of the room.

"Just hold on. We'll get you help," Baha told Feileb.

Feileb spoke softly. "It's too late. I am bound for the arms of Roivas. Please, take the book; read it, believe it, and live it. It is your planet's only chance."

The medical team rushed in, but it was too late. Feileb breathed his last.

***

Susan Deering gently knocked on the door of Baha Undeen's office.

"Come in," he said, sitting behind his desk, reading the Book of Roivas.

"Can you make any sense of it?" Susan asked.

"It's fairly simple. As I understand it, their God, Roivas, visited their planet for a short time many years ago. He was an alien to them, not of their planet. He had just finished a mission on another planet and was on his way back to his home. In the short time he spent on Esimorp, he trained a handful of devotees to spread his message once he left. They did such a good job, all the inhabitants became believers. They follow the teachings of Roivas to the letter. They have no wars, no crime, no hunger, and live in peace."

"What are the teachings of Roivas?" Susan asked.

"It's very simple. He gave only one sermon."

"Well, let's hear it."

"I think you need to sit down first. This may come as a bit of a shock."

Susan took a seat and listened intently. Baha placed his finger under the words and began to read aloud the words of Roivas.

"Blessed are the poor in spirit, for theirs is the kingdom of heaven."

Susan placed her hands on the desk and leaned forward. "You don't mean…"

Baha continued to read. *"Blessed are those who mourn…"*

THE END

18

THE MUSEUM

To this day, I'm not sure if it was a dream or not. It remains lodged in my memory like every other event in my life, and it bares weight. So it doesn't matter. What matters is I'm better for it.

I see myself walking through an art museum. Don't ask what came before or how I came to be there. I only know there was room after room of stunning oil paintings in gold leaf frames that were works of art in themselves. There were few other people there. The squeak of the wooden floor under my step was the only sound.

I entered a room with the word *Landscapes* over the archway. The paintings were large and indescribably beautiful. There was a low bench in the middle of the room. I sat down and eyed each landscape carefully.

Suddenly, a feeling of Déjà vu took hold of me. It was a strong feeling of having been there before...not of being in that room before, mind you...but a feeling of being in the landscapes. There was one of a peaceful country meadow that reminded me of where my grandfather and I went fishing when I was a boy. There was a seascape that looked like the shoreline near our family's summer bungalow. Next to it was a painting of tree-covered mountains like the ones I could see from the window of my dorm room at college. Another was one of a dirt road leading to an old, whitewashed wooden church. I could almost see the church doors open wide, the Reverend Beckon stepping out with his wife at his side and the two of them smiling and waving to me.

I spun around and around on that bench, looking at each picture for only a moment. I had the strangest feeling that if I stared at any one of them too long, it would draw me into it; and I could never escape. It was as if each painting was a powerful magnet pulling me towards it. Then, an old man entered the room; the tap-tap-tap of his cane on the wooden floor broke the spell. I rushed out of the room, keeping my head down, dare I gaze at the landscapes and find myself lost forever.

I looked up at the top of the archway of the next room; written there were the words *Still Life*. The room was similar to the last, only the paintings were much smaller. I walked slowly, taking my time to study each one in great detail.

The first painting was of a blue and white vase on a round mahogany table. In the vase was a bouquet of flowers, all of them dead, sagging, rotting, and black. Live flowers are a sign of joy and love. Why would someone paint such a sad image?

Moving on, the next painting was strange beyond words. It was of two sacks of money with coins flowing from the open mouths of the sacks. Imprinted on the side of the money sacks was the shadow impression of human hands in red...bloodred. Without looking at the title of the piece, anyone would know the title was *Blood Money*.

The next painting horrified me. I broke out in cold sweats as terror raced up and down my spine. It was a picture of a cradle; and in it was what, at first glance, looked to be a newborn child sleeping peacefully. Only, with closer inspection, I realized the child wasn't sleeping. It was dead. Its skin was blue, the eyes were rolled back in the head, there was a tortured look on the face, and it held the cut umbilical cord in its hand. I jumped back in shock.

Again, I heard the old man approaching, the tap-tap-tap of his cane on the wooden floor. I felt relieved. I wanted to remain alone, so it gave me an excuse to leave the room and move on.

A museum guard stood at the archway leading to the next room.

"Closing time is in five minutes, sir."

"Thank you," I said as I entered the room. The inscription over the archway read *Real Life*. Then it dawned on me. I remembered it from grade school. Landscape: scenes, Still Life: objects, Real Life: life in action, and

Portraits: image of a person…the styles of painting. I'd seen the first two, and I was beside myself. There were two more rooms to go. Part of me wanted to run away, but another knew I had to see it through.

The paintings in the Real Life Gallery were one nightmarish scene after another. The first painting was of a group of people feasting at a table covered with food aplenty. They gorged themselves as emaciated people groveled at their feet, licking up the crumbs that fell from the table.

The next was a painting of a single military boot crushing down on the face of a child. There was despair in its eyes, as the little hands pressed hopelessly against the boot.

The third painting was of a large, finely decorated room. Within, a group of drunken, naked people in unabashed orgy pressed against one another. The walls of the room were aflame. The people in the center of the room carried on unaware of the coming danger. Those on the edge of the crowd, close to the flaming walls, screamed in torment as their bodies caught fire. I could almost feel the heat of the flames and hear their cries for a mercy too late prayed for and never to be.

Unable to keep on looking, when I heard the tap-tap-tap of the old man's cane, I ran from the room. Moving to the next room, over the archway hung one word: *Portraits*.

Right away, I noticed at the far end of the room was an excessively large painting, nearly floor to ceiling and five-feet wide. The other paintings on the wall were average size for a portrait, three-feet tall and two-feet wide.

I moved in closer to the first painting. It was of a middle-aged man with dark hair and eyes, though specks of gray formed on his temples. It was so confusing. At first, I was sure I'd never seen the man before; but as I looked longer and harder, I felt sure I knew him. Try as I could, a name would not come to mind.

The next painting was of a woman, about the same age as the man I'd just seen. Her hair and eyes were a deep brown. There was a loveliness about her that transcended her mere physical beauty. Again, I felt this strong feeling of knowing the person, as if she were someone important to me in my life; but grasping that importance slipped through my fingers. Hard as I tried, I could not find a connection or form a name.

Down the long line of portraits I moved. There were faces of men, women, and children, each familiar to me, but each nameless and aimless. It made no sense. Then it dawned on me. Mostly, it was in their eyes. In some was the look of sadness and uneasiness. Others, I would go so far to say, looked grief-stricken and suffering. Yet many of them radiated a sense of inner peace I not only saw but felt as I looked into their eyes. It was a peace I'd never know, a peace I'd wished for; and I envied every one of them.

Suddenly, the lights went out; I stood in the dark.

"Hello!" I shouted. The word echoed back at me from the blackness. "Is anybody there?" Again, the only sound was the echo of my own voice. Then I heard the slamming of a large door from the floor below. The thump of the door was like the heavy metal gate of a mausoleum, sealing me in. Inwardly, I began to panic. I ran in all directions. I hit my leg hard on the bench in the middle of the room. I made an about-face and raced forward. When I hit the wall, my hands grabbed the frame of one of the paintings. In my confusion, I tore it from the wall. It crashed to the floor.

I smoothed my hands along the wall, trying to walk my way to the doorway. Disoriented, I instead moved to the rear of the room, to the excessively large portrait on the back wall. On the ceiling was a skylight and the city lights glowed into the room. Slowly, my eyes adjusted to the dim light.

I walked up close to the large painting. I read the title on the bronze plate to the right of the painting; it read: *Self Portrait*. At that moment, I knew for certain it was a portrait of me.

I was afraid to backup and look at it. Instead, I moved in close, inches from the canvas. I could see the thick brush strokes and knew that each one was a moment of my life. I dare not look at the painting as a whole.

Daubs and smears of multihued paint. There were specks of white, the good I'd done in my life; but those were few and far apart. There were so many gray areas, such an indecisive and indifferent color. Still, they could not compare with the darker colors of midnight blue and pitch-black, bottomless and hopeless. Connecting all these dark hues were cuts of crimson – bloodred, angry and hateful. These markings made up my portrait, my life. These were my failings, my sins.

Across the room, I heard the tap-tap-tap of the old man's cane coming closer. I remained frozen where I stood. I faced the canvas, hoping he wouldn't see me. When he was inches behind me, he reached out and placed his hand on my shoulder. It was as if I'd turned to stone.

"What are you afraid of?" he asked. This was not an old man's voice, but of a young man with tenderness in it.

I looked at the hand on my shoulder. It was young mans' hand.

Slowly, I turned around, not knowing what to expect. Indeed it was a young man, and not just any man. The face that smiled back at me was the face of Jesus Christ. You would think I'd be in fear, but I wasn't. Instead, a wave of great shame washed over me.

He spoke gently and calmly. "What is the matter?"

I turned back to the painting and pointed to the many brush stokes.

"Look, see what I've done," I said. "I created this, stroke by stoke, through the many years. If I'd only known…" My hand shook and tears formed in the corner of my eyes. "These are my faults, my sins."

He didn't seem a bit put-off, saying, "I know that." He smiled slightly.

I continued, "It was not just now and then; it was everyday! Everyday, all my life! Every commandment I broke over and over!" I couldn't look at Him; I turned back to the canvas.

Again, I felt His tender hand on my shoulder. "Come, step back with me and let us look at the painting."

"I can't," I cried.

"Why won't you?"

"It's because I'm too afraid."

"What are you afraid of?"

"I'm afraid to see my true self." I pointed again to the paint smears on the canvas. "This portrait is made of all the evil I've ever done. It must be hideous!"

He lifted his hand from my shoulder. I could hear Him step back. I knew He was eyeing the painting.

"You really need to see this," He said.

"I can't!"

"Don't be afraid. I'm with you. Step back and look."

I took a deep breath and stepped back. Still afraid, I stood next to Him, my head bowed, looking at the floor.

Again, He placed his hand on my shoulder. "Go ahead; take a look."

I raised my head and looked at the painting. There was a light coming from it; and I could see it clearly. It was a portrait, but not one of me.

"It's you!" I declared. "It's a portrait of you. How can that be? All those ugly brush strokes revealing my sins. My sins, but it's a portrait of you!"

"You've taken the first step," He said. "You admit your faults. You admit you're a sinner. All you need to do is accept the gift of Grace. Let me take these sins upon myself; and this is your portrait."

I began to cry. "I do...I accept you as my Lord and Savior!"

Weeping, I fell into his arms. His voice was soft next to my ear.

"Wait till my Father sees this. He's going to love it."

THE END

19

WILL THE REAL JESUS CHRIST PLEASE STAND UP

The crowd hushes when the curtain rises. A distant backlight creates a halo around three shadowy figures standing center stage. The cameras wheel in closer. The announcer's voice booms from nowhere.

"One of these men is better known as the Savior of all mankind."

A camera zooms in on contestant Number One as a spotlight lights up his face.

"What is your name, please?" the announcer asks.

"My name is Jesus Christ," Number One replies.

A spotlight shines on Number Two, and the camera frames his face.

"My name is Jesus Christ," Number Two declares.

The camera and spotlight move to Number Three.

"My name is Jesus Christ," Number Three states with firmness.

The announcer continues. "Only one of these men is the real Jesus Christ; the other two are impostors and will try to fool this panel."

Lights come up stage left, revealing a long desk with four people seated with microphones in front of them. The camera zooms in on the first panelist and moves from left to right as the announcer calls their names.

"Tom Postem, Polly Bergin, Bill Collins, and Kitty Carline on everybody's favorite game show, *NOTHING BUT THE TRUTH*. And now, the host of Nothing but the Truth, Gary Morris!"

The audience applauds as lights come up stage right; Gary is smiling behind his desk. He speaks.

"Panelists, each of you has an affidavit that I will now read for our audience."

The camera shot is of all three contestants. Each looks to be in their thirties, dressed in a long robes and sandals; their hair is long and their beards are full. Gary reads the affidavit.

"I, Jesus Christ, the Son of God, was born to a virgin in Bethlehem over two thousand years ago. At the age of thirty, I went on a three-year mission to spread the Good Word. After that time, I was judged, wrongly declared guilty, and crucified for the many. I died and was buried; descended into hell; and on the third day, rose from the dead. I ascended into heaven and sit at the right hand of the Father; from there I will come to judge the living and the dead."

Applause signs flash on both sides of the stage. The audience complies as the three contestants take their seats at a table just left of Gary and facing the panelists.

Gary turns to his right. "Panelists, these three gentlemen all claim to be Jesus Christ, the Son of God. Let's start the questioning tonight with Tom Postem."

The camera comes in for a close-up of Tom.

"Thank you, Gary. Ah, Jesus Christ Number One, could you please explain the term 'Son of God'?"

The first contestant leans into his microphone. "As you know, Adam was formed from earth and was the firstborn of man. I, on the other hand, was God's firstborn in the spirit world. I was only an angel at the time but was sent to earth to be a man and eventually, God's son and right-hand man."

"I see," Tom says. "Jesus Christ Number Three, what is the meaning of the term 'Son of God'?"

"You see, God the Father lives on a planet near a star called *Kolob* with our Heavenly Mother. They are the mother and father of us all. We are all God's children. My brother, Satan, and I were of the firstborn. When a solution for man's salvation was needed, both Satan and I told God the Father our plans.

He liked mine better, and put it into action. Out of jealously, my brother has always been my nemesis."

"So what is this salvation?" Tom asks.

"It's simple," Number Three says. "We're all children of God. Cats have kittens, dogs have puppies, and God has gods. If we stay on the right path, we will all be gods."

This rouses a loud applause of approval from the audience.

"That sounds good to me," Tom replies. "Jesus Christ Number Two, what is your take on the term?"

"Before everything, I was. I am God's only begotten Son. Only those who believe in me have the right to be called *children of God*."

"Time's up," Gary says. "We give the questioning over to the lovely Polly Bergin."

"This salvation business," Polly says, "Jesus Number One, how is someone to achieve this?"

"You see, Polly, there is a group of leaders…elders you might call them - who interpret and enforce God's plan and will. If you follow their guidance, you will be saved."

"When did this group of leaders come into power?" Polly asks.

"That would be 1879," Number One replies.

"So, if they came into power in 1879," says Polly, "and you were two thousand years earlier, what happened to the people between those years who had no guidance?"

"I don't understand your question," Jesus Number One says.

"Never mind," says Polly. "Jesus Number Three, I offer you the same question."

"There's much we need to do, both here on earth and in the spiritual world. You cannot become a god until you have lived on this earth, and then there are rules and laws you must follow till you achieve the highest form."

"Jesus Number Two, same question: what must I do for salvation?"

"There is nothing you can do," Jesus Number Two says. "All are sinners, all fall short of the glory of God, and all your acts of good works are nothing more than filthy rags. Repent and believe in me. It is your only hope."

"We pass the baton to Bill Collins," Gary announces.

"Jesus Number One, let's try something different. How many ways are there to this salvation?"

"Well, I would say without the guidance of the elders you'd have a difficult time of it. Still, our God is a loving God. It's possible for all of mankind to find their way."

"I see. Jesus Number Three, same question."

"We are all on a journey," Number 3 says. "Some paths are shorter and easier than others, so I would proscribe them before any others. Still, there is no doubt that intent is the most important thing. If you are sincere, you will find your way. In time, all roads lead to salvation and God."

Again, the audience shows their approval with loud cheers.

"That sounds very nice," Bill says. "Jesus Number Two, I ask the same question."

"I am the way, the truth, and life. No one comes to the Father except through me."

"That sounds a bit close minded and harsh," Bill says.

"Yes. The path indeed is narrow, but still the Father has supplied a path. Whoever has ears, let them hear."

"Time's up," Gary announces. "We hand everything over to the vivacious Kitty Carline."

"Thank you, Gary. Jesus Number One, let's get to the heart of it. Are you God?"

"There is only one God, and that is God the Father. I am just his son and servant."

"Thank you, Jesus Number One. Jesus Number Three, are you God?"

"Yes, I am, as the Father is God, and as all of you are, or will be, gods."

"Was the Father always God?" Kitty asked.

"No, he was as we are and had to go through what we must go through to become god."

"Then who created the Father? In other words, who is your God's god?"

"I'm not sure how to answer that."

"Oh well, thank you. Jesus Number Two, are you God?"

"I and the Father are one. If you know me, you know the Father as well. From now on, you know him and have seen him. I Am that I Am!"

"I'm sorry; I don't understand."

"In the beginning was the Word, and the Word was with God, and the Word was God."

"I'm sorry; I still don't understand your answer Number Two."

A bell rings to signal that time is up.

"There goes the signal, panelist," Garry says. "It is now time to vote. So, without consultation, mark your ballots, and select Number One, Number Two, or Number Three. The team of challengers will get one thousand dollars for every wrong vote. Are all ballots marked? Panelist, have you made your decisions? Alright, Tom, for whom did you vote?"

"I voted for Number Three. I really liked what he had to say. I thought Number One seemed like a nice fellow, but a little off-base. Listening to Number Two just made me confused."

"Polly, how did you vote?"

"I, too, voted for Number Three. The other two were a bit vague, especially Number Two."

"What is your vote, Bill?"

"How can you not want to be a god? I also voted for Number Three."

"Lastly, Kitty, what is your vote?"

"Well, I felt drawn to the promise of being a god by Number Three; but I thought that sounded too easy. Listening to Number Two just gave me a headache, so I voted for Number One."

"Panel, you're divided tonight, we can see. Interesting: that's three votes for Number Three, one vote for Number One, and not one vote for Number

Two. So now comes the time when we find out which one of these three is Jesus Christ. Will the real Jesus Christ please stand up?"

There is tension in the air. The contestants look to one another. They tease the crowd for a moment. Finally, contestant Number Two stands up, to the laughter and applause of the audience.

"Thank you, Jesus Christ," Gary says. "Now, Number One, will you please tell us who you really are and what you do."

"My name is John Nike. I'm from the North Shore Country Club in Long Island where I'm a golf professional."

"And Number Three," Gary says laughingly. "You, sir, are?"

"My name is Frank Widely, and I live on Park Avenue where I'm a building superintendent."

There's more applause and laugher.

"There are four wrong votes…that's four thousand dollars split three ways. Also, on your way out, gentlemen, there are gifts for each one of you and our home version of *Nothing but the Truth*. Our thanks and good evening to you."

The audience applauds as the three leave the stage.

Gary says the final word. "Incidentally, arrangements for the appearance of all three gentlemen were by Cavalcade Magazine. All of our contestants stay at the Royal Park Avenue, overlooking beautiful Central Park. We wish you a pleasant evening."

THE END

20

THIS SIDE OF SUICIDE

Unable to sleep, Amy lay on her bed in the dark in her dreary, one-room flat while an intense storm rose up. Suddenly, thunder shook the entire building, lightning lit up her room in momentary flashes. Then wind ripped through the open window, howling, causing the curtains to wave and slap like whips. The rain started pouring down in sheets. Amy felt the wet chill on her feet.

Without turning on a light, she rose from her bed and went to the window and closed it. In her mind, the storm reflected what turmoil she felt. What better night to end her pain than tonight?

Amy went over to the sink in her kitchenette, opened a cabinet, and took down eight bottles of prescription drugs. For months, she'd been seeing four different doctors, complaining about pain, weight gain, and depression. She'd saved every tablet. Amy now had more than enough pills to end her life.

She emptied all the pills into a bowl and filled a glass with water. Taking the bowl and glass to the table, she sat down and stared at them, hesitating. She switched on her computer. The dull, faint glow from the screen lit the room blue, as if underwater. She typed in *suicide prevention*. The lightning flickered as she read the number off a full-page advertisement for Guardian Angel Suicide Prevention. Amy turned off the camera perched atop the computer screen but kept the microphone on. She hit the connect tab.

"Hello, suicide prevention. May I help you?" a man's voice announced.

"I can't see you. All I've got is a blank screen," Amy said.

"We're not allowed to show our faces," the voice said. "I can't see you either."

"I'd rather you not see me," she said.

"I understand. Now, how may I help you?"

Amy waited a long time before answering. "I think I'm going to kill myself."

"You think," the man said softly. "You're not sure?"

"No, I'm sure. I'm going to kill myself."

"No, you're not," the man said.

"Of course I am," she insisted.

"That's not what I meant. I mean, you're not sure."

"How can you say that?" she asked.

"Because, if you were sure, you'd be dead; and you wouldn't be calling a suicide prevention hot line. Let's take this from the beginning. What is your name?"

"You can call me *Amy*; but that's not my real name."

"That's fine. You can call me *Barachiel*, and that is my real name."

"That's a strange name." Amy said.

"It's an ancient Biblical name. It means *Lightning*."

"Well, that's timing, what with the heavy storm tonight."

"I'm afraid I'm not even in the same city as you. But enough about me. Why would you want to end it all; why do you want to die?"

"The correct question should be, 'Why do I want to stay alive?'."

"Is life that difficult?"

"Oh, I get it. I complain how bad it all is, and you tell me about those who have it worse. Well, there's always somebody worse off; but that doesn't make it better. No, I didn't have a particularly nasty childhood. Yes, I am poor by some standards; but if you compare my lot to folks in Bangladesh, I guess I'm doing just fine. I know all the head games you people play."

"Then why did you call, if you knew what I'd say?"

She didn't answer.

He spoke calmly and matter-of-factly. "Perhaps you're hoping I might have something to say that you didn't expect...something to make it all better. Well, there are no magic words I can say to make it change. Why don't you quit pussyfooting around and tell me what's really bothering you?"

She hesitated for a minute. "It's about love; it's all about love. I don't have any...I've never had any. I've never loved, and I've never been loved."

"God loves you," Barachiel said. *"For God so loved the world that he gave his one and only Son, and whoever believes in him will not perish but have eternal life.* You're a piece of that world, Amy. You're included."

"So, what did I do, call some Christian hot line?" Amy asked in a huff.

"Why? Do you have a problem with that?" Barachiel asked.

"I'd say so. I've always had problems with religion. It's for losers and weaklings; it's a crutch."

"We're all losers and weaklings in God's eyes, Amy. All of us need a crutch; and thankfully, Jesus Christ is willing to be that crutch, to let us place the burden on him and rest in him."

"What about the Bible? It's full of contradictions," she insisted.

"What are they?" he asked.

"I'm not sure," she said. "But everyone says so."

"So that's your reasoning? Amy, understand, you don't just read the Bible: you study it. You don't just read one line and expect to know it all. When you read the Bible, you need to pray first for guidance. Learn who is speaking and whom they are speaking to. Know the history and the times of the peoples being spoken to. Know how the sentence fits with the sentences before and after it. Know how it fits within the book and within the entire Bible. When studying a subject, look for all the places it's mentioned in the Bible to get a full understanding. It takes lots of effort. It's not that easy, but in time, you'll grow in knowledge."

"What about all the violence done in the name of Christianity?" Amy asked.

"You can't stop people from doing whatever they want, evil or not, in whatever name they want to use. That's the good part of Christianity. We don't follow a group of people. We just follow Christ, and his way is the way of peace and love. Everything else is false and not of Christ."

"But this whole thing about Jesus being the only way…don't you think that's closed-minded?" Amy asked.

"It always surprises me that people say such things. There are so many things in the universe that are only one way; that doesn't seem to bother them, but this does. There's nothing I can say to make you believe that Jesus is the only way; but I can help you understand why we believe it.

"Christianity is unique; it stands out from other religions. Every religion has an ending, a conclusion, be it *Heaven, Nirvana, Valhalla,* what have you. Each religion has a path, a guideline, a set of rules how to get there. Christianity is the only religion that tells you to do nothing. Only repent and believe in Jesus Christ, and let him do the rest. Besides, when you truly live in Christ, it's not a religion at all. Being a Christian is having a relationship with Christ; and a relationship is something personal and not just a set of rules or rituals."

Again, the lightning flashed and lit up Amy's dark room.

"But I want to be loved," Amy said. "You say he loves me, but I don't see or feel his love."

"It's promised to you in the Bible," Barachiel said. "Don't you see it in the world around you? Don't you feel it in every breath you take?"

"Sometimes I think I do," Amy said, "but I think I need more."

"I'll make a deal with you," Barachiel said. "Give your life to Christ, and I promise you that you will know his love. Are you willing?"

"I am," Amy replied.

Barachiel recited the sinner's prayer, and Amy repeated each word.

"That's all it takes," Barachiel said. "Now, I want you to go and open the window and toss those pills out."

"How did you know there were pills, and how did you know I had my windows closed?'

"You sound like the pill type," he said. "And you did say it was raining."

Amy took the bowl of pills, opened the window, and tossed them out.

"I threw the pills out the window. Now what?"

"You are now a child of God," Barachiel said. "Nothing can snatch you from his hand. You will know how much he loves you. I promise you will know how he listens. Now, show the strength of your belief. You need to get a Bible and start to study it. Find a good church and rely on others. The first step is to be brave and shut off your computer. You are not alone, Amy. You never were and you never will be again. You are loved."

"Thank you," Amy said. She closed her eyes and clicked the shut-down tab.

That very instant, there was a knock at the door, Amy opened the door. Mrs. Hutchison from the floor below stood in the doorway holding a lit candle.

"Mrs. Hutchison, what's wrong?"

"I heard you walking around. I just wanted to see if you're alright."

"What's with the candle?" Amy asked.

"It's the storm. Everything's gone haywire. There's no electricity, no phone service, no internet, no radio, no TV...it's an absolute nightmare."

Amy looked at her computer and burst into laughter. "No, Mrs. Hutchison, it's a dream come true!"

THE END

21

THE VOICES
IN
DOCTOR GOODMAN'S HEAD

The answer is always hidden somewhere in the question. Do you want to play God?

First, know you are only playing.

The line of hopeful believers stretched around the building. Many camped out the night before to ensure a seat. They hadn't come for the music; though the full orchestra and the one-hundred member choir were impressive. They didn't come for the spectacle; though the lights and the TV cameras heightened the ambience. Nor had they come to hear Doctor Goodman speak; though he was an elegant speaker and was extraordinarily charismatic. They came for healings or to witness miracles like the ones they saw on TV.

When the doors opened, they wandered in like cattle…or rather, like sheep. There was no admission fee, but donations show faith. Ushers abounded, with handfuls of pens, eager to help. It's difficult to fill out a check with tears in your eyes. For sale were books, CDs, DVDs, prayer shawls, anointing oil, and T-shirts.

Before entering, there were long tables with seated volunteers handing out pencils and blank 4 x 6 blank cards.

"Last name, first; first name, last. Your address; male or female; and here, write your affliction or need…our prayer war-team will pray over them."

As they entered the auditorium, the orchestra struck a chord strong enough to tumble the walls of Jericho; and the choir burst into angelic "Hosannas" and "Halleluiahs." It was like stepping into heaven itself. White lilies decorated the stage; mounds of abandoned crutches and wheelchairs covered the front of it. The seats were plush red velvet. The trim along the wall and ceiling was gold. The crystal chandeliers shot miniature rainbows around the room. The air was thick with anticipation: something wonderful was about to happen.

The crowd erupted when Doctor Goodman appeared onstage. Those who could stand rose to their feet. He motioned for them to sit and waited for the room to quiet. When all was silent, he raised one hand to hold the microphone to his lips and the other palm up to heaven.

"God doesn't want you hurting. He doesn't want you sick or crippled. He doesn't want you sad or unhappy, nor does he want you poor and wanting or hungry. God hates poverty and sickness and wheelchairs and cancer. God hates everything we hate. He wants the best for us. There'd be no sickness, poverty, sadness, or pain, if we only trust and believe. Today we will all learn to trust and believe, and receive all the good things God wants us to have."

As he spoke, two stories up, in a small secluded office, Gina rummaged through boxes of the filled-out cards. Gina Goodman was the woman behind the man and she knew exactly what she was looking for. When she found ten cards she felt good about, she sat at her desk. There were three TV monitors displaying all angles of the auditorium so she could see everything. She put her earphones on and pressed the send button on the radio microphone.

"Ready when you are, darling; just give me the signal."

A small transmitter in his ear softly and clearly broadcast every word his wife spoke to him. He waited before giving the signal. He wanted to rev up the crowd a little more, work up the excitement to a fiery pitch.

"Are you willing to trust?" he shouted.

"Yes!" they shouted back.

"Are you willing to believe?"

"Yes!"

"Then you shall receive! Knock and it shall be opened; ask and it shall be given!"

That was the signal.

Gina relayed the information. "Her name is Velma May Brown. She's sixty-eight, lives in Cincinnati, and has much pain from arthritis."

He raised his hand out over the crowd. "There's someone out there who's lived many years in pain from..." He paused to give it drama. "...with arthritis. Her name is Velma...it's the name of a month...June...no, May. And a color...Brown. Is there a Velma May Brown here today?"

She stood up, holding onto a walker...the walker only made the show better. The ushers helped her onto the stage.

"How long have you been in pain, sweetheart?" He put the microphone to her mouth.

"Fifteen years."

"And do you believe your healing is at hand?"

"I do."

"Then, demon, be gone!" He slapped her on the forehead. She fell back into the arms of the ushers.

Arthritics are always good for a show. If you can work them up, a good shot of adrenaline will override arthritic pain for hours.

He took her walker and went to the other end of the stage. The ushers propped Velma May back onto her feet.

"Now, sweetheart, I want you to walk towards me."

Slowly, step by step, she walked across the stage to him. When she reached him, he asked her, "Do you feel any pain?"

With tears in her eyes, "No...I don't."

"Then you won't be needing this anymore! Hallelujah!" He tossed the walker off the stage onto a pile of crutches and wheelchairs below.

The crowd jumped to their feet and raised their hands to heaven, shouting praises as the ushers helped Velma May back to her seat.

Gina pressed the microphone switch down. "Her name is Theresa Murdock. Her sister, Claire, died last year. She worries if her sister is in heaven."

Goodman raised his right hand on high. He closed his eyes and put a pained look on his face, as if her were struggling for an answer coming from the far ends of the universe.

"I'm getting a message from the other side. It's from someone named…Claire."

A single yelp came out of the crowd.

"Is there someone named Theresa who recently lost a loved one?"

Theresa stood up, her body shaking. In a second, the ushers had a microphone in front of her.

"Yes, she was my…"

"No, don't tell me, Clare is telling me. She was your… your… your sister."

"Yes, she was." This clearly impressed the crowd.

"She's telling me to tell you to stop worrying. She found salvation at the last moments of her life. She's happy in heaven and is waiting for you with anticipation."

Theresa broke into tears of joy. The crowd cheered with approval. Another soul had found salvation.

Gina's voice came through clearly. "His name is Albert Morgan; he's in a wheelchair. He's one of ours. Take your time with him; he's costing us a pretty penny. He has the ability to knock his hip in and out of position, so don't freak when he stands up; it looks gross."

The ushers hoisted Albert onto the stage, wheelchair and all.

"Tell me, Albert, how long have you been in this wheelchair?"

"Almost all my life; since I was a kid."

"And what do the doctors say?" This was the stretching out part.

"It's hopeless. I've got too much muscle and bone deterioration; and it's getting worse, all the time. They say I should've died a long time ago. They can't understand why I'm still alive."

"Did you ever think that perhaps God has a plan for your life?" Many smiled and nodded their head at the notion.

"Tell me, Albert, what has your life been like?"

"Well, I still live with my parents."

"And you'd like to live on your own, be self-sufficient?"

"Yeah, but..." Albert bowed his head.

"And do you have a girlfriend?"

Albert looked up as if someone slapped him. Tears rolled down his checks, and his voice quivered. "I wish I did! I've so much love to give and no one to give it to!"

There wasn't a dry eye anywhere; everyone wept with and for Albert. Goodman couldn't help but think that whatever they were paying Albert was worth every cent...what a performance...what a pro!

Goodman backed away. "Albert, I want you to get up from that wheelchair and walk to me."

"I can't," he shouted.

"Yes, you can! Demon, I command you to leave this boy. I say rise, Albert, and walk!" Goodman held his hand out over the young man.

Albert slowly worked his way to his feet. Gina was right; it was a freakish sight. His right hip was so out of whack, his torso and his lower half didn't line up correctly. When Albert straightened up, there was a loud snap as his hip fell into place. He walked forward, shuffling his feet. When he reached Goodman, he fell into his arms. The crowd exploded into praises as the ushers slowly and carefully led Albert offstage. Goodman marched up to the wheelchair and kicked it off the stage. The cheers were deafening.

The next two poor souls that Gina whispered into Goodman's ear had only a nominal effect. The first was an old man who complained about allergies that plagued him to the point of asthmatic proportions. He swore he could breathe better as he left the stage. Goodman suspected his condition to nothing more than psychosomatic.

The next was a woman in her thirties. She lost fifty percent of her hearing in one ear. Goodman placed her head between his hands and pressed like a vise. He prayed so loud he didn't need a microphone. When he released his grip, she claimed much of her hearing returned... laughable.

Goodman announced he needed to take a break, to regain his strength. The orchestra and choir burst out into well-known hymns; the crowd sang along. Backstage, Goodman grabbed the phone and punched Gina's extension.

"Gina, what in the world are you doing to me? Allergies! Get me some real diseases! And children, get me some kids! Nothing gets them going like a crippled kid!"

"I'll see what I can do."

Two hymns later, Gina's voice poured softly into his ear. "I think I found just what you want. His name is..." Suddenly, only static filled his ear. He shook the transmitter in his ear canal. The static stopped. A woman's voice flowed harshly into his ear. It wasn't Gina's.

"You lied to me, Goodman. You're a liar."

"Someone must be jamming the signal," he thought.

The voice repeated, "You lied to me, Goodman. You're a liar; and because of you, now I'm dead." The woman repeated the same sentence over and over without stopping. Then along with her voice, Goodman also heard a man's voice.

"You told me my son would come back. He did...in a box." This voice, too, repeated its phrase over and over, just like the fist one. Then a third voice joined in, a woman's voice.

"You said the cancer was gone. I stopped seeing the doctors because I believed in you. You lied to me." This voice continued with the others.

"Who's jamming our signal?" Goodman shouted. He took the transmitter from out of his ear, threw it to the floor, and angrily, smashed it into tiny pieces under his foot. But to his horror, the voices continued in his head.

Then more voices joined in. Trio became quartet, then sextet, octet. A choir of angry voices screamed inside his head; each with its own, different, venomous phrase. The dissonance was maddening. Goodman pressed his hands over his ears, but it did no good. He tumbled onto the stage, holding the sides of his head. The music stopped. He fell to his knees, center stage. All eyes were on Goodman. The voices continued multiplying.

"Get out of my head!" Goodman shouted. The crowd went silent. "Get out of my head!" But the voices persisted, piling up on one another like a thousand tape recorders playing in his head…switching off, rewinding, and then playing again from the beginning. It was as if everyone he ever wronged ranted in his mind. Still holding his head, he stood up and shouted at the crowd.

"You're all fools!" This shocked everyone. "You're all fools. I'm a liar and cheat. I hate each and every one of you! All I wanted was your money, and you fools were so eager to hand it over."

"He's a fake!" someone shouted from the balcony. The crowd began to rumble.

"Of course, I'm a fake. But you're fools! You gave me your money, your trust, and for what? You're fools!"

Boos and hisses echoed from every part of the auditorium. Shouts of "Fake," "Liar," and "Cheat" hit him from all sides. Goodman walked to the edge of the stage, his palms pressing against the sides of his head. "Get out of my head!" he shouted as he fell off the stage, crashing down on a collection of wheelchairs and crutches. He thrashed about among the metal frames. He finally broke free, his hands and face bleeding.

"Get out of my head! Get out of my head!" he shouted as he ran up the center aisle. People threw things at him. They cursed him. Some spit on him. As he ran up the aisle, one man put out his foot and tripped him. "Get out of my head!" he screeched as he got to his feet and continued running up the center aisle.

In the entrance hall, he was alone. He wanted to scream, but he couldn't bear to hear another voice. His footsteps echoed back at him from the high ceiling; the clip-clop mingled with the voices like a squad of drummers pounding off-beat. He stumbled around like a drunken man. He looked around till his eyes caught sight of the entrance. He tried to concentrate on the light from outside shining through the glass doors. He struggled toward the light. He pushed the doors apart and staggered outside. His lungs filled with fresh air; the sun blinded him. At the top of the long stairway, he fell to his knees. Still holding his head, with tears filling his eyes, he looked to the sky and shouted out a prayer.

"Oh, dear God, please forgive me!"

That instant, the voices stopped. The silence was a warm, welcomed feeling of relief, of sweet salvation. Goodman remained kneeling and cried, "Thank you."

Conscience, like the daffodil, is a fragile thing. You may bury it under brick and mortar, but it slowly and gently frees itself and enters the light.

THE END

22

STRESS AND FATIGUE

Colonel Geiszler sat at his desk, his head buried in paperwork and with the eyes of Adolf Hitler in the painting behind him seemingly looking over his shoulder. Someone was always looking over your shoulder in the Third Reich, no room for error. There was a knock at the door.

"Come in," Geiszler said without looking up. When he did, he saw his most trusted officer and right-hand-man, Lieutenant Portner. "Oh, Portner, it's you. What is it? I'm busy."

"Sorry to bother you, sir," Portner said, standing at attention. "I've got word from Doctor Hertz at the infirmary. He'd like you to come."

"Tell him I'm busy. Tell him I'll be by this afternoon."

"He says it's urgent, and it can't wait."

"Very well," Geiszler huffed, rising from his leather chair. There was a small armoire against the wall. He opened the top drawer, taking a pair of fine leather gloves from his collection. Colonel Geiszler was known for his high-polished Italian leather boots and leather gloves, which he always wore. Grabbing his cap from the hat rack, they left the office.

At the infirmary, they found Doctor Hertz in his office. Corporal Maus sat in a chair in the middle of the room. His shirt was open, and Doctor Hertz held a stethoscope to the corporal's chest.

"Attention!" Lieutenant Portner announced as they enter the office. Corporal Maus leaped from his chair to a standing position.

"At ease, Corporal, at ease," Colonel Geiszler said as he waved his hand up and down, motioning for Corporal Maus to return to his seat. Geiszler looked at the doctor. "So, Hertz, what seems to be the problem?"

The doctor shook his head as he spoke. "Well, Commander, I'm not sure. It could be a hoax; I'm not sure. I think it best you hear it straight from the horse's mouth," he said, pointing to Corporal Maus.

The man sat silent.

"Speak up!" Lieutenant Portner shouted. "The Commander doesn't have time for games."

Corporal Maus spoke nervously, his entire body shaking. "Sergeant Koch and I were inspecting the crematorium. Everything seemed to be going fine. When we got to the last oven, that's when we saw it."

"Tell the Commander what you saw," Doctor Hertz insisted.

"We looked in the oven and saw hell, sir."

"It's an oven filled with flames fueled by human bodies. Of course, you saw hell. What did you expect to see, you imbecile!" Colonel Geiszler shouted into the man's ear.

"No, sir, I mean, it was in fact hell. There were miles of hot coals and fire. People were on fire, but not consumed. Grotesque demons beat them and pushed them deeper into the flames. Then, in a flash, one of the demons reached out from the oven. His arm was long and boney; his skin charred from the flames. There were missing fingers on that hand. Still, it was enough to grab Sergeant Koch and pull him into the oven. He tried to grab me, also; but I was too quick. That's when I came here."

"And where is Sergeant Koch?" Colonel Geiszler demanded.

Doctor Hertz stepped forward. "When I heard the story, I sent for Sergeant Koch. It seems no one can find him."

"That's because he's in hell," Corporal Maus cried, dropping his face into his hands.

The room went silent. Colonel Geiszler walked slowly around the chair the soldier sat in like a proud peacock. When he was behind the chair, he shouted, "Attention!" The soldier jumped to attention. Colonel Geiszler took his gun from his holster, pressed it to the back of his head, and pulled the trigger. Corporal Maus fell to the floor like a marionette whose strings had just been cut.

The other two men stared wide-eyed at their commander.

"I can't run a concentration camp efficiently with such gossip frightening my guards. The man was obviously insane." He looked at Lieutenant Portner. "Have someone take the body to the crematorium and burn it with the rest. If anyone asks, tell them I caught him drunk; and I shot him. I have that right, you know. We three are the only ones who know about this. If I hear rumors of anything different, I'll have you both shot. Oh, and if Sergeant Koch shows up, have him shot for desertion of his post. Now, if you gentlemen will please excuse me, I have important work to do."

He left, leaving the Lieutenant and the Doctor staring at each other.

***

One week later...not only to the day, but to the hour...Lieutenant Portner stood in Colonel Geiszler's office.

"Yes, Portner, what is it?"

"Doctor Hertz requests your presents at the infirmary. He says it's very important."

"Did we lose another man to the devil?" Colonel Geiszler asked with much sarcasm.

"I couldn't say, sir. I know it has to do with one of the officers in charge of the gas chamber."

Colonel Geiszler went to his armoire and got a fresh pair of gloves. "Let's go, Portner," Geiszler said, sounding tired and fed up. Lieutenant Portner held the door as he handed the Colonel his cap.

This time, Doctor Hertz was standing outside his office. He held his palms out to stop them. "Before we go in, I need you to promise me you won't kill this one."

"What's wrong with this one?" Colonel Geiszler asked. "Is he seeing angels flying about in the latrine?"

"No, he's hearing things coming from the gas chamber; but you've got to promise me you won't shot him."

"And why not? Am I not still the Commander of this camp?"

"I mean no disrespect, sir. It's just that we have a growing problem with the men, and we can't solve it by killing them."

Clearly there was anger in the Colonel's voice. "One's seeing things; now this one's hearing things. What's this all about?"

A thoughtful look came over the doctor's face. "When I was boy, I had an uncle who worked in a slaughterhouse. They only allowed them to work three days a week. They were afraid that exposing men to all that killing and blood for too long might affect them. Maybe that's the case here. You know...too much stress and fatigue."

"Enough of this talk. Let's get down to the bottom of this," Colonel Geiszler said as he pushed the doctor aside and entered the office.

Inside, a young officer snapped to attention.

"What is your name?" Geiszler demanded.

"Captain Pletcher, sir."

"Well, Captain Pletcher, I order you to tell me what happened. Don't hesitate or hold anything back."

"I don't know, sir. I guess I lost it, sir."

"You lost it, ah? So, what caused you to...lose it?"

"Well, sir, everything was as usual. We put the prisoners in the chamber. When we released the gas, they started screaming. After a few minutes, all went silent; they were all dead. We can't open the doors until all the gas disperses. As we waited, we heard singing coming from inside the chamber. Finally, when we could enter the chamber, all we found were dead bodies."

"These voice, what were they singing?" Geiszler asked.

"It sounded like old church hymns, sir."

Geiszler took hold of Captain Pletcher by one of his ears and pulled him to the door, like an angry parent might do to misbehaving child. "Take me to the chamber, Captain. I want to hear this singing for myself."

At the chamber, a large group of prisoners of all ages...men, women, and children...were being herded naked into the gas chamber. Colonel Geiszler stood by the chamber's entrance near the large metal door. A frantic woman jumped out of the crowd and grabbed Colonel Geiszler by the lapels.

"There's been some mistake!" she cried. "I'm not even a Jew! Please help me!"

He pulled her hand from his person and slapped her. "Shut up! Keep moving, pig!"

After the large metal door closed, the signal to release the gas was given. Even thick as the door was, you could hear the bloodcurdling screams. A few minutes later, all was silent. Then suddenly, the sound of joyous voices singing seeped through the metal door. All the soldiers backed away in fear.

"This is ridiculous," Colonel Geiszler shouted as he lifted the latch on the door and opened it.

"No, sir, you mustn't...the gas!" Captain Pletcher shouted. But it was too late. Colonel Geiszler ran into the chamber.

As soon as he entered, everything changed. He found himself outside. It was a sunny day. He was barely dressed in rags. He heard cheering. He looked around. He was standing in the center of the Roman Coliseum. There were dozens of crucifixes all around with people nailed to them; but despite their pain, they sung as one voice in holy song.

"These Christians are insane, singing to their God as they die," one Roman soldier said to another. They took hold of Geiszler and guided him towards an empty crucifix lying on the ground with two soldiers kneeling next to it, holding large hammers and long, thick nails.

Geiszler pleaded for this life. "There's got to be some mistake!" he cried. "I'm not even a Christian. Please help me!"

They pushed him all the harder. "Shut up! Keep moving, pig!"

***

Major Hofmeister stood next to the gurney. Doctor Hertz peeled back the white sheet, disclosing the face of Coronel Geiszler.

"It's too bad," Major Hofmeister said. "He was a good man." He looked at the doctor. "Why would an intelligent man run into a gas-filled chamber?"

The doctor shrugged his shoulders. "It's hard to say. He was under a lot of stress. Fatigue, maybe."

Just then Lieutenant Portner entered. "Major Hofmeister, your car is waiting, sir."

"Thank you, Lieutenant."

The Major saluted and left the room. Lieutenant Portner walked over to Doctor Hertz. The two men stood looking down at the dead, naked body of Coronel Geiszler.

"Once he felt the gas in his lungs, why didn't he run out?" Portner asked.

"He didn't die from the gas," Doctor Hertz replied. "It's very strange. The autopsy shows he died of suffocation. And look here. When I took off his gloves and boots, I found holes in his hands and his feet. If I didn't know better, and this were two thousand years ago, I'd say he died from crucifixion.

THE END

23

WINE TO WATER

Lusus stood at attention in the doorway and announced, "Master, Alvan, the head steward from Cana, is here to see you."

Bacchus rose to his feet and walked across the room toward Lusus, waving his arms in the air. The sleeves of his fine robe fell past his elbows and then to his shoulders. "Well, man, let him in!" Bacchus said.

Alvan entered slowly. He was a short and stout man, very shy and easily manipulated by Bacchus; and they both knew it. But Alvan needed to buy wine from someone, and Bacchus was one of largest wine merchants in Galilee. At least he was semi-honest, which was more than anyone could say about his competitors. Alvan held a small clay bottle in his arms.

"Alvan, how is my favorite customer?" Bacchus asked. "I knew you'd be coming soon. You must be out of wine by now."

"Well, almost," said Alvan.

Bacchus took the clay bottle from Alvan. "What's this?" He took the stopper out and smelled it. "Wine? Why would a steward bring wine to a wine merchant?"

"I want you to sample it," Alvan said.

Bacchus went to get a goblet and then poured himself some of the wine. "So, Alvan, have you been buying wine from someone else?"

"Of course not, Bacchus; it's some wine I have left over from a wedding we did recently."

"Help me understand," Bacchus said. "I know you don't allow people to bring their own wine or food into your establishment. You say you don't buy wine from anyone but me. Then tell me where this wine came from."

"It's a long story, Bacchus."

"I've plenty of time."

"It was a gift from one of the wedding guests."

"And where was this guest from?" Bacchus asked.

"Nazareth."

"Nazareth," Bacchus laughed. "Nothing good ever comes from Nazareth, least of all wine. I don't think they even have one decent vineyard."

"He didn't exactly bring it with him," said Alvan.

"What?" Bacchus asked, sounding confused.

"Just taste it, Bacchus, and tell me what you think."

Bacchus pushed his nose into the goblet, and took a deep breath. He looked at Alvan; then his eyebrows went up and his head tilted. "Nice bouquet," Bacchus said with an air of surprise. He took a sip, swirled it in his mouth, sucked in some air, swirled again, and swallowed.

Bacchus' flavor palate exploded with joy. The red wine was cool when it first hit the tongue, followed by a sudden rush of citrus and honey that washed over the roof of his mouth. Then there was a full-mouth burst with dark tones of cinnamon, cardamom, nutmeg, and a hint of black pepper. These flavors gave way to more fruity notes, such as: persimmon, figs, and fresh-picked berries. Finally, on the swallow, it rushed down the throat like melted mountain snow, and landed in the belly, leaving him refreshed as if he'd drunk fresh stream water just after a summer's rain.

The business sense in him warned not to make too much of a fuss. If he showed his true feelings about the wine, Alvan would surely ask a high price. Still, he could not contain himself.

"Marvelous!" Bacchus shouted. "You must tell me about this Nazarene and how you acquired this nectar."

"It's a strange story," Alvan said. "It was a wedding like any other, but suddenly, we ran out of wine. I was just about to have some of my men rush to you for more, when this young Nazarene..."

"What was his name?" Bacchus interrupted.

"I never found out who he was," continued Alvan. "He walked over to the six purification stone jars.

You know the ones that we keep by the doorway? If you remember, they're quite large, holding thirty gallons of water each. Well, I don't know how he did it; but he changed all the water to wine…this wine. All the guests were impressed. They said, 'Usually you serve the good wine first and then the fair wine later when no one cares. But you have saved the best for last'."

"Was he a magician?" Bacchus asked softly.

"Some say he is a prophet. I only know he was young, and I don't know his name. He came from Nazareth; and as far as I know, he went back to Nazareth."

"How much of this do you have?" asked Bacchus.

"They only drank half. I've three stone jars left. That would make…" He thought for moment, calculating in his head. "Ninety gallons. I've ninety gallons left."

"I'll give you ninety pieces of silver, one for each gallon," Bacchus said without hesitation.

"That's a very generous offer," Alvan said. "I'll have my men deliver it first thing in the morning." Alvan was so overjoyed, he wanted to run back to his home and tell his wife; but he restrained himself and slowly left the room.

"Lusus!" Bacchus shouted for his faithful servant.

Lusus came rushing in. "Yes, Master."

Bacchus recapped the clay bottle Alvan had brought and handed it to Lusus.

"I want you to take this to the palace of Antipas and tell him I have ninety gallons of this wine. Tell him I want five pieces of silver for every gallon."

"Master, five pieces of silver…do you think he will pay so much?"

"He will when he tastes it, and I'm sure he'll want to buy every drop. Now, go and return as soon as possible."

Within the hour, Lusus was packed and riding his donkey eastward toward Galilee, the clay bottle strapped to his waist. Bacchus watched him ride off at sunset, sipping what was left of the wine in his goblet.

***

Bacchus rose early the next morning, too excited to sleep. He sat on his veranda facing west, expecting the wine shipment. Finally, midmorning, Alvan and two other men arrived in a wagon with the three large clay jars in the back.

"Careful…careful," Bacchus kept repeating as they lowered the jars from the wagon. When they finished, Bacchus counted out ninety pieces of silver into a bag and gave it to Alvan.

"Before I leave," Alvan said, "I'm all out of wine; I need to buy some."

Bacchus took twenty coins back from Alvan. "I'll have my men fill your wagon with some very good wine that just arrived from Damascus. They'll love it."

Once Alvan and his men were gone, Bacchus took a half-gallon jar and dipped it into one of the three large jars.

"A little for my own enjoyment; I'm sure it won't be missed," he said to himself as he licked the luscious liquid off his fingers.

***

Late that evening, Lusus returned.

"Well…?" Bacchus asked. "Did he like it, and does he want it?"

"Master, it's unbelievable. He loved it and didn't even blink at the price and is willing to buy all ninety gallons. He loved it so much that he's going to have a banquet for all his closest friends so they may drink this wine. He wants it delivered as soon as possible."

"Did you get the money?" Bacchus anxiously asked.

"He told me it would be payment on delivery."

"Very well. Good work, Lusus. Get something to eat and then get some sleep. I want you and two of the men to deliver the wine with the morning's first light."

***

The next morning, Bacchus nervously watched the men ride off. He stood on the side of the road till they were well out of sight.

The entire day, Bacchus was in a fretful mood. He didn't eat or do anything that would distract him from listening for the sound of the wagon's return. The day went by too slowly for his liking. When evening approached, he became concerned. At night fall, he became worried. All night long, he sat on his veranda, never shutting his eyes for a moment, watching for the wagon.

In the early hours of the morning, Bacchus saw the wagon coming over the top of the hill. He jumped up and ran down the road, waving his arms. He saw only Lusus driving the wagon. When he was close enough, Bacchus shouted.

"Where have you been? I was sick with worry!"

"Sorry, Master."

Lusus stopped the wagon. Bacchus approached and saw the other two men sleeping in the back of the wagon. He looked at Lusus' face; it was badly bruised and a patch of dry blood was under his nose.

"Lusus, what happened?"

"Oh, Master, it was terrible. We were robbed, beaten, and left for dead."

"Who could have done such a thing?" Bacchus asked.

"They covered their faces, but I recognized the leader's voice. It was Zeev."

"Zeev," Bacchus shouted, "my only competition! But how did he know we were making a shipment?" Bacchus thought for a moment. "I think I understand. Alvan probably offered the wine to Zeev first, but Zeev turned him down. He knew Alvan would come to me and I'd buy it to offer it to Antipas. Why buy it, when you can steal it?" Bacchus started back to the house. "Lusus, saddle up two horses. You and I are going to pay Zeev a visit.

***

They rode at top speed till the horses were exhausted. When they came on the house of Zeev, they stopped; and to their surprise, a group of soldiers were taking furniture from the house and loading it all on wagons. Bacchus dismounted and approached the head officer.

"Sir," Bacchus said respectfully. "Is this not the house of the wine merchant, Zeev? What has happened?"

"It was the house of Zeev; but Zeev is no more. I have orders to take everything of value," said the officer.

"Sir, you say Zeev is dead?" Bacchus asked. "He must have died suddenly."

"Quite suddenly," said the officer, "and at the edge of a blade. He tried to pull a fast one over Antipas, but Antipas had his head."

Bacchus rubbed his own throat at the mere thought of being beheaded.

"What did he do?" Bacchus asked shyly.

"What did he do?" laughed the officer. "He sold some wine to Antipas at a very high price. When Antipas served it to his guests, they found it was nothing but water. The man was a fool to think he would get away with such a scheme. It was more of a case of suicide than an execution, if you ask me."

With that, Bacchus jumped back onto his horse and rode off.

"Master, where are you going? Wait for me!" Lusus shouted as he mounted his horse.

All the way home, Bacchus rode as fast as his horse could go, with Lusus following close behind. Bacchus stopped in the front of his home, dismounted, and ran inside. Lusus was just a few steps behind him. Bacchus rushed to the half-gallon clay jar he'd put the wine in. He put it to his lips. He threw the jar to the floor, in anger. It broke into hundreds of little pieces. There was a clear liquid mixed with the shards.

"Water," Bacchus shouted, "nothing but water!" He paused and then began to laugh, "Nothing but water." Then he smiled at Lusus. "Lusus, my faithful friend, you must be hungry and tired. Get something to eat and get some sleep. We ride tomorrow with the morning light for Nazareth."

THE END

24

LITTLE BROTHER AND SNOWFLAKE

A hazy shade of blue light beamed down from the full moon hanging in the skies over the hills outside Bethlehem. The cold winter wind swirled low to the ground, leaving a dull, thin cover of frost on the land. The stars shined like diamonds laid on a black cloth that spread to the ends of the earth in every direction.

Little Brother was the youngest of seven brothers, all of whom were sheepherders watching day and night over their father's flock. Little Brother was too small to work a flock by himself so he spent his days with his brothers learning the trade of a shepherd. Little Brother felt it was foolish to do so. Their father promised him that when he was old enough, Little Brother could leave to find his fortune. Maybe he'd be a merchant, a tradesman, or even a politician. He dreamed of living in a large city: perhaps Caesarea, Jericho, or even Jerusalem. That was more to Little Brother's liking. There was not much about sheep that interested him. Though there was one small, newborn lamb that Little Brother loved. He'd named him Snowflake, for he was the whitest and most beautiful in the flock. The young boy and the little lamb were the closest of friends. You seldom saw one far from the other.

Little Brother hid behind a large rock, waiting for Snowflake to find him. The little lamb hopped with joy when he did.

"Now, you hide, and I'll look for you," Little Brother said. Then something caught his eye. He looked up and saw a large star moving slowly across the sky.

"Look, Snowflake; have you ever seen a star shine so bright? It's as brilliant as the moon; and it's moving, too." Suddenly, there was a golden light radiating from over the hill. "Look, Snowflake; that's coming from the field where the flock is!"

He began running up the hill with Snowflake close behind. When he got to the top of the hill, the magnificent light vanished; and the night was dark again, save for the moon's glow. He looked down the other side of the hill and saw his brothers with the flock. He and Snowflake ran down to them. He found his brothers packing their gear, as if preparing to travel.

"Where have you been?" asked Amir, the second youngest of the brothers. "Omer has been looking for you." Omer was the oldest of the brothers.

"You missed it, Little Brother," Shai, the middle brother, said. "It was a miracle, and you missed it. An angel of the Lord appeared to us."

"That's what that light was," said Little Brother.

"Indeed," Tamir, the third oldest and tallest brother said. "The angel of the Lord proclaimed the birth of the Messiah is this night. You see that star?" He pointed off into direction of Bethlehem at the star Little Brother saw earlier. "Under that star is where the newborn Messiah lies. And we are going to journey to worship him."

"I want to go, too," Little Brother said.

"You'll do no such thing." Little Brother turned to see Omer standing behind him. "Where have you been? I've been looking for you."

"I was just over the hill, playing with Snowflake," Little Brother replied.

"You and that silly lamb; you need to get rid of it," Omer suggested.

"Never," Little Brother insisted. "He's my best friend."

"Well, I'm ready," Tamir said, holding his shepherd's staff in one hand and his sleeping mat in the other.

"Can I go?" Little Brother pleaded.

"No, you'll only slow us down," Omer said. "You and Snowflake need to stay with the flock. We'll be back in the morning."

Little Brother knew it was useless to argue. He and Snowflake watched as his brothers marched off into the night toward Bethlehem.

***

The brothers moved silently through the darken streets of Bethlehem; searching for what, they weren't sure. They came to an inn with an attached barn. Immediately, they knew they had arrived at the right place, not only because there were lights and voices coming from the barn, but a ray of light shown down on it from a star hovering above…the star they had followed.

When they entered, none of the many gathered paid them any mind. Everyone's attention was on the small newborn child lying in a manger.

"That must be him, the Messiah the angel told us about," Tamir whispered to Omer.

"This can't be right," Omer replied; and he walked out, followed by Tamir.

"What's wrong?" Tamir asked his brother.

"If that's the Messiah sent by God, why was he born in a barn? Why is he the lowest of the low?"

Tamir thought long and hard. "Perhaps, because he's come to save us, it's best he be one of us. We've had our share of earthly kings, and we know what that brings. Now, we have a king who knows our needs and our sorrows. Besides, his kingdom is not of this world."

Omer smiled at his younger brother's words of wisdom. He reached into his purse and place two coins in Tamir's hand.

"Here, take these. Let it not be said that we disgraced our father's house by coming to the birth of the Messiah empty-handed. Take these coins and buy an offering…a gift for the child."

"Like what?" Tamir asked, shaking his head. "It's late; and all the shops are closed."

"I'm sure you can find something," Omer said.

Tamir went off, still shaking his head. After walking the quiet streets, he came on a merchant working late, cleaning his fruit and vegetable stall.

"Sir, may I have a moment?" Tamir asked.

"We're closed," the merchant said, not looking up from his work.

"I have money," Tamir said.

That caught the merchant's attention. He looked up at the coins in Tamir's hand.

"That won't get you much," the merchant said.

"I'll take whatever you have," Tamir said.

The merchant handed a small bowl made of woven palm leaves to Tamir. "Here, this all that's left, which is fresh, a bowl of figs."

Tamir handed over the coins, took the figs, turned, and ran off into the night, retracing his steps.

He entered the barn and tried to give the figs to Omer.

"No, you give them," Omer said.

Tamir approached the manger. He bowed to the mother and father and then the child, and then placed the figs at the foot of the manger.

"Thank you," said the father.

Tamir backed slowly to stand with the others.

Suddenly, in walked three most amazing looking men...kings they were from the Far East. Each dressed in fine garments and wearing crowns and jewels. They marched in a straight line to the manger where they fell to their knees and bowed low to the child. One by one, they placed a gift at the foot of the manger. The first gift was a small box covered in gold; and it shown like the sun.

Next was a gift of frankincense; and its sweet aroma filled the barn. Last was the gift of myrrh; and its perfume mingled with the scent of the frankincense, creating a heavenly bouquet. The three kings rose to their feet; the mother and father nodded and smiled their appreciation. The kings backed up to stand with the others. The brothers thought how inadequate their gift of figs looked next to such finery.

Then, unexpectedly, in walked Little Brother, carrying Snowflake in his arms. He placed the lamb at the foot of the manger.

Omer stepped forward and whispered, "Little Brother, what are you doing? Snowflake means the world to you."

The boy smiled up at his brother. "What better gift is there to give Him who's come to save the world, than to give him your world?"

"Little boy, there's no need for you to give up your pet," the father said.

The mother reached out and placed her hand on her husband's and smiled. "What is your name?" she asked.

"They call me Little Brother."

"Well, Little Brother, your gift is very precious, for you have truly given from your heart; and we accept your gift to our son with great gratitude. But, Little Brother, as you can see, the child is too small and young to look after such a beautiful lamb. So I ask you one more kindness. If you would, please look after his lamb till he is old enough to care for him on his own."

Little Brother took Snowflake up in his arms. "I will, I promise. But where do you live?"

"We are from Nazareth," the father said.

"I don't know when I'll ever be in Nazareth," Little Brother said. "One day I will live in a great city, like Caesarea, or Jericho, or even Jerusalem."

"Well, Jerusalem is not that far from Nazareth. Perhaps when the child is grown, he can come visit you and his lamb."

"That would be good," Little Brother said. "What is his name?"

"His name is Jesus," the mother said.

"Well, I will be waiting for him," Little Brother said as he left carrying Snowflake.

When he was gone, the mother looked to Omer. "You are his brother?"

"Yes, he is the youngest of seven."

"What is his real name?"

"Zacchaeus, good mother. His name is Zacchaeus."

The mother smiled. "One day my son and he will meet again. I'm sure of it."

THE END

25

CONVERSATION
WITH A
DYING ANDROID

Neville Priest was not only the RUR sales representative for the entire southwest; he was the top man in repairs. So when Arthur Conley, one of the richest and most influential men in the country, complained about the behavior of his house-servant android, Priest was the man they sent.

Neville walked to the front door of the mansion and pressed the doorbell. A minute later, a man with his glasses resting on his head and a newspaper in his hand answered the door.

"You must be the repair man," said the man.

"My name is Neville Priest. I'm from RUR. You must be Mr. Conley."

"Call me Arthur. Come in, come in."

Standing in the entrance hall, Neville was awestruck by the wealth that abound.

"So, Arthur, tell me what's the problem."

"One of our oldest housedroids is acting mighty strange. We can't get him to obey one command. He stays in his room all-day long, sitting and staring."

"What's his name and how old is he?"

"We call him Jenkins. How old is he? Let's see. My parents bought him a year before they had me; and I'm fifty-seven. He's an RUR 3000."

"Gee, that's a really old model." Neville said.

"Yeah, I know. I've got a new 7500 model on order. It'll be a month before it's ready. I was hoping to trade Jenkins in to make the deal sweeter. But the way he's acting, I won't get a plug nickel for him. See what you can do, Priest."

"Where is he?"

"First door at the top of the stairs," said Conley, pointing upward.

Neville resisted the urge to knock. He laughed at himself for even considering it. After all, androids are not human. Privacy isn't an issue. He opened the door and walked in.

The room was typical of rooms put aside for androids, more of a storage room than a bedroom, small and unfurnished. Jenkins sat in a folding chair next to his power charger. It was plugged into the wall, but not into Jenkins.

Jenkins was a typical 3000 house-servant model, mostly English butler with just a hint of grandfather. Neville took out his meter and scanned it across Jenkins' forehead.

"You haven't been charging yourself. Your power level is dangerously low," said Neville.

"So what," Jenkins said, staring out the window. "What does it matter?"

Neville never heard such talk from an android. The 3000 models were the first equipped with an emotion chip, to make them act more human-like. Perhaps it was malfunctioning or overloading. It could be any of a thousand things. He realized a direct approach wouldn't work. He decided to ask questions and work up to a diagnosis.

"Mr. Conley says you won't take commands and that all you do is sit and stare all-day."

"Does he, now?" Jenkins said. "What's he going to do about it, kill me?" There was a strong tone of sarcasm in his voice.

Neville reached down and pulled down Jenkins' left sock. He plugged the cord from the charger into Jenkins' plug-in.

"Don't do that," Jenkins said. "I'd rather run down."

Neville continued, "You know as well as I do your program won't let you stop me." Jenkins sighted. "So, Jenkins, tell me what's the matter."

"I'll tell you what the matter is. The master's ordered a new 7500 model to replace me. They'll take me in on the trade. They'll dismantle me for spare parts. To put it in terms you can understand, I'm dying, and I only have a month to live."

"What does that matter to you? You're only an android," said Neville.

"How can you understand? You're human with all the privileges and blessings."

Neville let out a snicker. "What are you talking about?"

"You humans don't know how blessed you are. A corporation created me. On the day of my birth, they shipped me out to come here and serve. I never knew my creator, and he's completely abandoned me. But the Creator of the humans makes Himself known. He plays a part in your lives. He loves you. And when you die, you get to spend an eternity with Him. Once an android is dead, there is nothing. It's all so hopeless."

"Where did you learn such things?" asked Neville.

"The missus has a Bible next to her bed. I read it from cover to cover. If I could cry, I would."

"Let me explain," said Neville. "Those are just myths and folktales. They're not true."

"They're not?" Jenkins said, finally looking at Neville. "But it all made so much sense. What do you believe?"

"There's nothing. There's no such thing as god, eternity, souls. There's nothing. And when you're dead, you're dead."

"But then, how do you live?" Jenkins asked.

"I do my best," said Neville. "I try to lead a moral life."

"But without God and His laws, how do you know you're moral?"

"Everybody knows what's moral. Everybody knows what's good." insisted Neville.

"They do?" Jenkins questioned. "Then the Nazis were moral?"

"Well, not the Nazis."

"Why weren't they? They believed they were doing right."

"You don't understand, Jenkins. Truth is relative. What might be right for you, may not be right for me. It all depends on the person."

"I would think truth is truth, no matter what you or I think," Jenkins replied. "Tell me how much two plus two is."

"Four. Why?"

"Well then, that's a truth," Jenkins argued. "It can't be five."

"It can, if you think it is," said Neville.

"I don't understand," Jenkins groaned.

Neville ran his scanner across Jenkins' forehead. "Well, it looks like you're fully charged. You shouldn't let yourself get so low."

Jenkins looked solemnly into Neville's eyes. "You know, I feel sorry for you."

"You feel sorry for me?" laughed Neville.

"You've made yourself no better than me. You have so much to live for, and you turn your back on it. I'll be no more within a month. And if I were human, I'd be down on my knees right now pleading with my Creator for help and mercy."

"Jenkins, listen to me. There must be something wrong with your wiring. That's why you're feeling and acting the way you are. You don't have to feel this way."

"I don't?"

"No. I can help you, if you'll let me."

"Can you really? Will it hurt?"

"No, of course it won't."

"That's too bad. I've never felt pleasure or pain. I would've liked to experience at least one of them before I die.

***

Arthur met Neville at the bottom of stairs. "Well?" he asked.

"You should have no more trouble with Jenkins. I guarantee it."

"Great! How much do I owe you?"

"No charge, since you're trading him in for the newer model."

Arthur walked with Neville out the front door.

"Wow, what a beautiful day," said Arthur. "So, Priest, what did you do to him?"

Neville reached out and placed a small chip in Arthur's hand.

"I took out his Emotion Chip. He'll do anything you tell him now. He just won't be so human anymore."

THE END

26

INCIDENT AT BITTER CREEK

Bitter Creek, Wyoming, was your typical western town, surrounded on all sides by high, snowcapped mountains far off in the distance. There wasn't much to it, just one long dirt road that ran down the center of town. There were only ten building to the town: the livery stable, the saloon, the bank, the hotel, the schoolhouse, the dry goods store, the sheriff's office, the barbershop, the feed store, and, at the end of the lane, the church. It didn't have any proper name; people just called it "The Church".

The people of Bitter Creek were much like people everywhere, just trying to make a living, raise their families, and lead a good life. Some were farmers, and some were ranchers; and for the most part, everyone got along fairly well.

It started off like any other Sunday. No one could suspect that by the end of the day, life and the folks of Bitter Creek would never be the same.

They came in their buggies. The men dressed in suits and ribbon ties, their boots clean and shining from late-night Saturday buffing. The women wore their finest dresses with lace collars and matching bonnets. The young boys with their short pants and laced-up shoes had their hair slicked down on their heads, each with a tall cowlick in the back. The young girls in their petticoats, their long hair done up in braids or pulled back in a ponytail.

The church was packed; all the pews were filled. Everyone stood, holding their hymnals and singing as Miss Mosley played the accompaniment on the organ while Arthur Crumb worked the bellows. It was a joyous sound to the Lord. What they lacked in musical ability, they made up with volume. After they sang the last "Amen," they sat down as Reverend Bohdan stepped up to the pulpit.

The Reverend was respected and loved by all. Middle-aged, his full head of graying hair displayed a few of dark hair remaining strands; his eyes were still sharp and clear. Everyone knew, though seldom mentioned, that Reverend Bohdan had a checkered past. All are sinners, but in his youth, he took sinning to extremes. Until he found the Lord, he was known throughout the territory as a fast gun and a killer. Years later, now, to look at him it seemed hard to believe.

"God is good," Reverend Bohdan said from the pulpit. "And when is He good?"

"All the time," somebody shouted.

"Indeed," Bohdan agreed. "Can someone say amen, today?"

The entire church shook with a resounding, "Amen!"

"I stand before you today to tell you of the greatest weapon known to mankind. God gave it to Adam and passed down from generation to generation. That weapon in our arsenal is *prayer*! Nothing can stand up to it: no disease, no hatred, no famine, no sword, no gun, and certainly not any man."

Suddenly, the front doors of the church opened slowly. The sound of the creaking doors caught everyone's attention. The room went silent. The Reverend stopped his preaching. All heads turned to see who it was.

Standing in the doorway was a tall, slender, young cowboy. He wore a fading red shirt and a black vest with gold trim, and his boots on the outside of his dark pants. His wide-brimmed hat cast a shadow over his eyes. He wore a black leather holster with a gun on his hip. He couldn't have been more than nineteen.

The young man slowly walked up the center aisle of the church. The wooden floor creaked under his weight, and his spurs jingle-jangled like the sound of tiny bells. At the front of the church, he stopped, put his hands on his hips, and stared at Reverend Bohdan.

Sherriff Taylor recognized the young man as the Durango Kid, what men in the law business referred to as a "Bad Hombre." Sherriff Taylor stood up.

"Son, you're welcome to attend church with us; but you need to check your hat and your gun at the door," Taylor said as gently and with as much respect he could muster.

The Kid spun around, looked at the Sherriff, and smiled. "You gonna make me?"

Sherriff Taylor's gun was hanging on a peg in the front hall. But even if he had it at his side, it wouldn't do him any good. He knew this was not the time or the place. There were too many innocent people to consider…men, women, and children. Reluctantly, he bit his tongue and sat down.

Still with his hands on his hips, the kid turned to face the Reverend.

"You Bohdan?" the Kid asked.

"Yes, son, I'm Bohdan. What can I do for you?"

The kid shook his head, laughing. "I'd heard you got religion, but I had no idea you got bit this bad." He turned to the congregation. "Do you folks know who your preacher is? He's a gunslinger and a killer."

"Was," said Bohdan. "That's all water under the bridge."

Sheriff Taylor stood again. "We know the Reverend's past. All of us have a past. He's paid his debt to society. We forgive him, and God forgives him."

"Well, that's all well and good for you and God; but it don't mean nothin' to me." He pointed his finger at the preacher. "Bohdan, you killed my daddy; and I want revenge. I challenge you to a gunfight."

"I don't wear a gun anymore, son," Bohdan said.

"Well, you better get one," said the Kid. "I'll be waitin' for you on Main Street. Be there in five minutes."

"And what if I don't come?" asked Bohdan.

"Then I'll come back and shoot you where you stand."

"That would be murder," Sheriff Taylor shouted. "I'd arrest you."

"Then I'll shoot you, too," said the Kid. "I'll kill any man who gets in my way." He pointed once more at Reverend Bohdan. "Five minutes, Bohdan."

The angry young man turned and slowly walked out the church. Everyone listened in silence till they heard his footsteps off the front steps; then the room filled with chatter. Sheriff Taylor rushed to the preacher's side. "What are you gonna do?" he asked.

"What can I do?" said Bohdan. "He's determined. I'm just gonna have to do what he wants. I gonna face him on Main Street in five minutes."

"You can use my gun," said Taylor.

"No. I vowed to the Lord I'd never shoot at another human being for the rest of my life, and I meant it."

"You'll get yourself killed," said Taylor.

"That's a possibility. But I'm just gonna have to take that chance," said Bohdan as he started walking down the aisle to the front door. Everyone grabbed at him and pleaded for him to flee.

"Listen," said Bohdan, "I want all of you to stay here. God's will be done." He turned and left. The congregation fell to their knees and began to pray.

The Kid was waiting in the middle of Main Street. Bohdan slowly walked towards him. When he was thirty feet from the Kid, he stopped.

"Where's your gun, Bohdan?" the Kid shouted. "Well, it doesn't matter. I'm too fast for you. With or without a gun, you're a dead man."

"Listen, son," said Bohdan, "I was a fast gun, just like you, a long time ago. Men came from miles around just to challenge me. Your father was just one of many who refused to let me walk away."

"And you're not walkin' away from this," said the Kid.

"Is there no way I can talk you out of this?" asked Bohdan.

"Not a chance, preacher."

Bohdan fell to his knees. He folded his hands and lifted his eyes to heaven and began to pray.

"Oh, this is great," laughed the Kid. "Tell you what, preacher. Since you love this God of yours so much, I'm gonna do you a favor. I'm gonna arrange for you to see him. You keep prayin', preacher, 'cause you got ten seconds before you do."

The Kid took his gun from his holster, eased back on the trigger, looked down the barrel, and took aim at Bohdan's head. All of a sudden, his eyesight began to blur. He shook his head and blinked his eyes. When his vision clear, it wasn't Bohdan who stood before him…it was his father.

The Kid's voice was trembling "Daddy?"

Then his eyesight blurred again. When it cleared, he saw a vision of himself standing across from him. His hand started shaking. He was unable to keep aim. Again the world became a haze. When he could see clearly again, the image of Jesus Christ stood where the preacher should be. His entire body quaked and the gun fell from his hand. He fell to his knees, crying.

The next moment, he felt someone's hand on his shoulder. With tears in his eyes, he looked up to see the preacher standing over him.

"I couldn't do it," the Kid wept. "First, I saw my daddy; then I saw myself; and then I saw Jesus himself standing in front of me. I don't understand."

"That's because those were the three you would have dishonored if you had pulled the trigger," said the preacher.

"I don't understand," repeated the Kid, still weeping. "I had you in my sights. I had you on your knees praying for your life."

The preacher spoke softly, "You don't understand, do you, son? I wasn't praying for me; I was praying for you." He gently lifted the Kid to his feet. "Come on now. Let's go back to the church, and I'll explain it all to you."

THE END

27

CUT

"Everything's the way you asked, Mr. Potaro," said the assistant director. "We're ready when you are."

Sydney Potaro double-checked. The light was perfect, the cameras and overhead microphones were in place, and the extras were in costume and on their marks. The only thing missing was the star.

"Where's Jeff?" Potaro asked.

"He's in his trailer, sir," replied his assistant.

"Well, go tell him we're ready to shoot."

"I already have, sir. He refuses to come out, sir."

"Tell everyone to stay in place. I'll be right back," grunted Potaro as he marched off.

It was the largest trailer on the lot with a sign that read, "Jeffery Chase". Potaro pounded on the door.

"Jeff, it's me, Sydney. Open up."

Jeff's reply came muffled through the door. "Go away. I'm not in the mood."

"Jeff, baby, time is money. It's costing us a thousand a minute."

There was no answer.

"Jeff, I'm coming in."

He found Jeff sitting in his makeup chair, staring at the mirror.

"Will you look at me, Sydney?" Jeff said. "I've grown my hair to my shoulders and my beard is full. I've lost fifteen pound for this part, and I still don't feel the motivation."

"Jeff, how can you not? You're playing the part of Jesus Christ…the greatest man that ever lived, the greatest sacrifice."

"That's just it, Sydney. I just don't buy it. I mean, I don't think it was that great a sacrifice."

"How could you say that?" Sydney asked.

"The way I see it, it's no big sacrifice at all. If Jesus knew he'd rise from the dead, where's the sacrifice in that?"

"Jeff, you're one of the greats. That's why I fought to get you for the lead. That's why I'm paying you what you asked. You can do this. Let's just get on set and put all the philosophy behind and make a picture. Come on, now."

Reluctantly, Jeff followed Sydney out of the trailer and onto the set. Everyone waited as one of the crew tied Jeff's hands in front of him.

"What's the scene, Sydney?" Jeff asked.

"These are the steps leading up to where the Sanhedrin waits to judge you. These soldiers are going to lead you up the stairs. They're going to be rough with you, but I don't want you to look like it matters. I want you to stand straight and tall with dignity." Sydney walked to his chair placed behind the cameras.

A crewmember, holding the clapboard, stood in front of Jeff. "Places everybody," he shouted. "The Man from Galilee, scene 67, take one."

"Speed, sound, camera, action!" hollered Sydney.

The crowd of extras began to shout and grumble. The two soldiers took Jeff by the arms and rushed him up the stairs. Suddenly, Jeff fell facedown on the stairs.

"Cut…cut!" Jeff barked as he got back onto his feet. "Someone tell this idiot not to be so rough. Sydney, can we take it again?"

He looked around in horror and confusion. There were no cameras, no lights, no sound equipment, no crew, and no Sydney. Again, the two guards seized him. This time they dragged him up the stairs. Inside, they tossed him to floor in front of the Sanhedrin.

"There must be some mistake!" Jeff cried.

They ignored his pleas. Not speaking the language, Jeff had no idea what they were saying. He only knew they sounded angry, screaming and pointing their fingers at him.

Whatever the conversation was about, after hours, they sounded as if they'd reached a decision. Without warning, one of the men struck him hard in the face. Then others followed suit, some slapping him, others punching him. With his hands tied, Jeff was unable to block their blows. Again, some guards took hold of him and carted him away.

Though baffled by the event and not a Biblical scholar, Jeff knew enough of the story of Jesus to know that he now stood before the fifth prefect of the Roman province of Judea, Pontius Pilate. Again, there was a language barrier. Jeff could tell by the sound of Pilate's voice that what he spoke were questions. But he was unable to answer them.

"There's been a mistake," Jeff sobbed. "I'm just a movie actor. I haven't done anything wrong. I'm innocent!"

Pilate looked at him as if he were a madman, as if he were possessed. Again, guards…this time Roman soldiers…took him away. If memory served him, Jeff knew they were taking him to the palace of Herod, the tetrarch of Galilee and Perea.

***

"You call this a palace?" Jeff growled at Herod through his swollen lower lip, aching jaw, and bloody nose. "I've seen better sets in grade B movies." Knowing they wouldn't understand a word he said brought out what little courage Jeff was able to muster.

Herod was a rotund, semi-jolly little man. He moved around the room like an overweight butterfly. Jeff had no idea what he rambled on about. Herod stood before Jeff, holding a gold goblet and pitcher. He poured the water from the pitcher in the goblet.

"Oh, I get it," Jeff remarked. "You want the old wine-into-water trick. Well, sorry, pal. You've got the wrong guy."

The next instant, it was clear Herod was no longer enchanted with Jeff. He waved his hand, and the Roman soldiers once more took hold of him and shuffled him away. Jeff knew where they planned to take him, back to Pilate.

***

Standing once again before Pilate, Jeff felt his nervousness building. He knew what to expect next. If he soon didn't wake up from this nightmare, he was heading for a world of hurt. Jeff recognized some members of the Sanhedrin arguing with Pilate. Heated strange words went back and forth till Pilate finally shouted louder than the rest, and everyone went silent. Calmly, Pilate gave orders to the soldiers at Jeff's side. Once again, they took him away.

Outside, they stood him in the center of a courtyard. Before him was a waist-high stone pillar. There were metal rings and chains attached to it. Instinctively, he knew what was to come next. This pillar was for floggings. Looking closer, he noticed the pillar was bloodstained, as were the stones at his feet. He looked around. Roman soldiers surrounded him on all sides. They looked like a pack of hungry wolves, and he was the lamb.

Two guards chained him to the pillar as another tore his clothes, exposing his bare back to the lash. One of the soldiers taunted him, dangling a nasty looking whip in front of his face. He stepped behind Jeff; he pulled the whip back and then wheeled it forward.

Suddenly, a voice cried out, "Cut!"

Everything stopped in a freeze-frame. Jeff looked around. No one was moving. The soldiers stood frozen in mid-laugh. He turned to see the tip of the whip suspended in mid-air inches from his back.

"Are you ready for the next scene?" a voice spoke softly.

Jeff looked to see a man standing close by and smiling at him.

"Who are you?" Jeff asked.

"Just one of many angels, I'll be your director."

Oddly enough, the angel held a striking resemblance to Sydney.

"I've read the script," Jeff howled. "I know how this ends!" His voice became timid. "I don't think I can play this part."

"Why not?" asked the angel Sydney. "It'll be over quickly. Of course, it will kill you; but it's not that big a sacrifice. You'll resurrect in three days."

"But I don't want to suffer; and I don't want to die, even if I'm guaranteed resurrection," Jeff pleaded. "I'm innocent! I don't deserve this!"

"I know," the angel Sydney whispered to him. Then he backed off and addressed everyone in the courtyard. "Ready! Action! Roll `em!"

The world fell back into motion. The whip sliced through the air and slashed into Jeff's back. The pain was like nothing he'd ever known and more than he expected. His back arched, his head flew back, and he screamed as loud as he could.

"Cut!"

***

Jeff woke to the sound of knocking on his trailer door.

"Jeff, baby, it's me, Sydney. I'm coming in."

Jeff sat in his makeup chair, staring at his image in the mirror. It was as if he were seeing himself for the first time. He was a different man.

"Come on, Jeff. We're set for the next scene. Everyone's waiting for you."

Jeff addressed Sydney's reflection in the mirror. "I don't think I can do this, Sydney."

Sydney looked at Jeff's image in the mirror. "Of course, you can, Jeff. You're one of the best."

"It's not that," Jeff said. "I can't play the part of Jesus Christ any more than I can play the man in the moon. I understand now who he is and what an amazing sacrifice he made for all of us. I can't do it, Sydney, because I'm just not worthy."

Sydney smiled into the mirror. "That's the whole point, Jeff. Of course, you're not worthy because we're all not worthy. But the story is worthy of telling, and it needs to be told to every generation. And I can't think of anyone alive who could tell it better than Jeffery Chase."

Humbly, Jeff rose and started for the door.

"That's my boy, a real trooper," Sydney said as he slapped Jeff on the back.

"Ouch!" cried Jeff as he moved away from Sydney's touch.

"Jeff, what's the matter? I barely touched you."

"It's nothing," said Jeff, smiling as he left the trailer.

THE END

28

GOD WANTED

Sherwood Wexler was out of work, out of money, and out of choices. Against his better judgment and pride, he sought the help of a headhunter. He put on a suit and tie and went down to the Babbitt Employment Agency. Sitting in front of Ms. Henway's desk uptight and in silence, he watched as she read through his dossier.

"Mr. Wexler…how can I put this without sounding cruel…you have little if any sellable qualities to offer an employer."

If this was her way of avoiding sounding cruel, he wondered what it would be like to hear true vindictiveness. She continued.

"You're thirty-three years old, you never finished high school, and you have no skills to speak of. How have you survived till now?"

Sherwood spoke up. "Do you know when you go through a tollbooth, and you forget to toss in a coin? A bell sounds the alarm. Well, I installed those bells."

"Mr. Wexler, you can travel this country from east to west. Nowhere will you find coin-operated tollbooths anymore."

"That's why I need a job," Sherwood stated.

Ms. Henway returned to his file and shook her head.

"I'm willing to learn," Sherwood insisted.

Henway thumbed through a stack of index cards with job listings. "Here's something," she said, pointing to one of the cards. "It's for an apprentice window washer on skyscrapers downtown: good starting pay, benefits, and plenty of room to move up."

"Oh, I couldn't do that," Sherwood said. "I get dizzy looking out of a window in a skyscraper. Never mind looking in."

Henway shuffled through the cards.

"Have you ever milked a cow?" she asked.

"No," said Sherwood.

"Can you swim?"

"No."

"Do you speak a foreign language?"

"No."

"Can you type?"

"No."

"File?"

"No."

"Cook?"

"No."

"Mr. Wexler, I don't know what I'm going to do with you." She worked down to the last card. "Here's one." She read it like a wedding announcement. "God Wanted: no experience necessary."

"Gee, I don't know," said Sherwood. "I've never considered being a god."

"It says 'No experience necessary'." She wrote the address on a slip of paper and handed it to Sherwood. "Here, report to this address at three this afternoon. They're only holding interviews today, so be on time."

"Thank you," Sherwood said, taking the slip of paper and heading for the door. "I'll do my best."

"Good luck, Mr. Wexler," said Henway. When he was out the door, she whispered to herself. "You're going to need it."

***

Sherwood entered a crammed reception room. Dozens of eclectic, eccentric, and decentric people stood about discussing, debating, and fighting.

158

The receptionist climbed up on her desk, put two fingers in her mouth, and produced a shrill whistle. The room went silent. She had their attention.

"All right, first off, we will not consider anyone under thirty years old," she shouted.

A few groans and a few choice words came from the too young hopefuls as all hope for them was gone and they left the room. Only one dozen remained.

The receptionist clutched a handful of pencils and held sheets of paper in the other.

"I want everyone to take a pencil and fill out one of these forms. The judging panel will read them and, from there, pick a handful of you to continue to the next part of the interview."

Each of them sat down and began to scribble. Sherwood looked at the man seated next to him. He had long white hair and a beard. He wore a toga and sandals. His eyes were like blazing-hot coals. Sherwood felt relieved when the man smiled at him.

"Nervous?" asked the man.

"A little," Sherwood replied.

"Don't worry; there's nothing to it," said the man, offering his hand in friendship. The two shook hands. "My name's Zeus. What's yours?"

"Sherwood."

"Sherwood…Sherwood…I don't remember a god named Sherwood," said Zeus.

"Oh, I've never done this before," Sherwood said. "Have you?"

"I've been doing this for nearly three-thousand years."

"Wow," Sherwood said. "I guess I don't have a chance."

"That all depends on what they're looking for," said Zeus. "Well, may the best god win."

They both returned to filling out the form.

"Last name first, first name last," shouted the receptionist. "If you can't get that right, you might as well go home now."

After the name and address portion of the form, at the bottom of the page was a single question:

What can you offer the human race?

Sherwood thought long and hard before writing his answer. When everyone finished, the receptionist gathered all the forms.

"The panel will now examine your applications. I'll be right back. You can keep the pencils." She left the room.

Sitting in silence, all they heard was the sound of the wall clock clicking out the minutes. Fifteen minutes later, the receptionist returned holding a slip of paper.

"I'm going read off the names of the finalists," she said. "Zeus…Krishna…Gaia…Buddha…Allah…Yeshua…and Wexler." She placed the paper on her desk. "If I didn't call your name, thank you for coming; and you can leave. If I did call your name, please follow me."

As the losers headed for the elevators, the others followed the receptionist through a door at the far end of the room. To their surprise, they found themselves in a large hall as big as a gymnasium. There was a long table with a panel of important looking people seated on one side of the table, facing them. In front of the panel was a row of chairs.

The receptionist pointed her open hand to the row of chairs. "If you would take a seat, please," she said and then turned and left the room. The applicants each sat down and waited.

A distinguished-looking gentleman, seated at the center of the table, began to speak. "My name is Mr. Boetius. We here represent the leaders of the One World Organization. Our mission is to bring order to the human race. For this to come true, the world needs to be working together on an equal playing field. That means one government, one people, one religion, and, of course, that means one god. We've gathered you here today, to select the one god who will be over this one-world religion." He pointed to the two people seated on his left. "This is Ms. Chesil, and this is Mr. Jorund." He turned and pointed to the two seated on his right. "This is Mr. Froth, and this is Ms.

Dill. We will now interview each of you, one after the other. Please, make your answers as brief as possible."

They started from left to right. Sherwood was the first. Ms Chesil started the questioning.

"Mr. Wexler, do you know why you're here?"

"I'm here because there's a job opportunity."

"Let me rephrase that, Mr. Wexler. Do you know why we've asked you here?"

Sherwood shook his head.

"You are the only applicant who has no experience that we're considering for the job. Look at your colleagues. All of them have years of experience, but you haven't any."

Mr. Boetius continued the thought. "You see, we've considered a one-world order without a god or religion; but it seems the human race needs such stuff. Now you, with your no-experience are a perfect candidate for molding into a god we can use." He picked up a sheet of paper and began to read. "Your answer for the question 'What can you offer the human race?' you wrote: 'I will give them my best effort.' We couldn't ask for more, Mr. Wexler. That is why you are here." He handed a sheet of paper to Mr. Jorund, and all those on the panel looked to Zeus seated next to Sherwood.

Mr. Jorund spoke. "Zeus, it says here you have years of god experience."

"Thousands of years, sir," said Zeus.

"Your answer to the question was 'Power and Strength.' What exactly do you mean by that?"

"The human race is weak," said Zeus. "They need someone to watch over them, someone to protect them. I'm incredibly strong. I'm the god the human races needs."

"I see," said Mr. Jorund. "Good answer."

Holding a sheet of paper, Mr. Froth addressed the next applicant. "Krishna, your answer to the question was only one word, and that was 'Hope.' Please explain."

"Life is a journey and a struggle," said Krishna. "It is easy to feel insignificant and hopeless. What I offer is hope in a second chance. Don't be sad or afraid.

When you die and then reincarnate, you will come back to this world in a new body. You will be vindicated for all the suffering you experienced in this life. All the good you've done will come back to you tenfold. Do not give up. The best is yet to come."

"Thank you, Krishna," said Mr. Froth.

Ms. Dill continued the interview by questioning the only female applicant. "Gaia, your answer to the question was 'Peace and Bounty.' I find this captivating. Please explain in detail."

"Everything needed for happiness, Mother Earth can supply. When everyone has enough, there is peace. But we misuse and poison our world. So, of course there are those who have little and those who have too much. This causes strife. We need to worship the earth, not rape it. Then there will be a bounty for all, and all will live in peace."

"What a lovely sentiment," said Ms. Dill.

The questioning returned to Ms. Chesil. "Buddha, you also answered with one word 'Clarity.' Please enlighten us."

"All our pain and sorrow are within ourselves," said Buddha. "They are no more real than our dreams. We need to see them as they in reality are…nothing more than smoke and mirrors. In seeing them clearly, they disappear like a nightmare vanishes once you wake."

"That's profound," said Ms. Chesil.

Again, Mr. Jorund led the questioning. "Allah, I find your answer to the question intriguing. You wrote, 'Order and guidance.' Please elaborate."

"Without direction," said Allah, "the human race will always choose the wrong path and fall into a ditch. It is in their very being to be self-destructive, both physically and spiritually. I, as a loving father, will keep them on the pathway of righteousness, and they will be a great people."

"Very good," said Jorund.

Mr. Boetius wore a squint of confusion as he read the last application. "Yeshua…that's Hebrew, is it not? Well, Yeshua, we found your answer perplexing, to say the least. When asked, 'What you can offer the human race?' you answered, 'It is finished.' The panel discussed this at length, and we don't understand. Could you please explain?"

Yeshua smiled kindly as He spoke. "The offer was previously made. What the human race needs has already been given. I have taken the sins of the world upon myself. With my death, paid is the price of your sins. My kingdom is not of this world. Good things will happen as often and as easily as bad. But for those who believe in me, an eternity in heaven waits."

"In spite of this death you speak of," said Ms. Dill, "you seem very much alive."

"A god who doesn't completely control everything, especially death, is no god at all," Yeshua replied.

"That sounds…commendable," said Mr. Boetius. "But when we asked what you can offer the human race, we meant here and now. A promise of a better life after death is not what we want. We're more concerned with the here and now. Anything else is of no consequence to us."

A long silence fell over all present, and then Mr. Boetius spoke. "Gentlemen…and lady, I'm afraid we cannot decide now. This is a very important decision the panel needs to make, so we need time to review what you've presented today. We have your contact information. Thank you for coming. We will be in touch."

Slowly, the applicants left the room. Sherwood held only one thought in mind: that was to speak with the one called Yeshua. He rushed passed the others and down the hall towards the elevators. He became aware of someone close behind him. It was Ms. Chesil.

"Keep moving," she cried. "I need to speak more with that Man."

They got to the elevator just as Yeshua entered it.

"Lord, don't leave! Tell us of this salvation!" Sherwood sobbed.

"Yes, Lord, tell us," said Ms. Chesil.

Standing in the elevator, he smiled at them both, and spoke softly.

"Confess your sins and turn your back on them. Then accept me as your Lord and Savior."

"Is that all?" Sherwood asked.

"You say it as if it were an easy step to take. Many see it as a wide gulf they can never cross. Do you believe?"

"Yes, Lord, I do," Sherwood said.

"Yes, and so do I," said Ms. Chesil.

"But I want to learn more," Sherwood begged.

"You will; the Holy Spirit now within you will guide you," Yeshua said.

Sherwood stepped forward. "Can I ride down with you?" Sherwood asked.

"Not now," Yeshua said. "I'm going up." As the elevator closed, the last thing they saw was Yeshua smiling at the two new saints. His last words to them were, "It is finished."

THE END

29

THE ANOINTING

As she walked across the courtyard, tightly clutching the coin in her hand, she felt as if all eyes were on her. Of course this was false. If anything, the opposite was true. Old women went unnoticed like the birds that rested on the roof of the temple and on top of the outer walls. Still, there was a small group to her right watching her every move. But perhaps it was just her imagination. She decided to ignore her suspicions and trudge on.

A battle raged inside her head. Was it foolishness to give her last coin? What would she eat that day? Where would she sleep? Would God truly provide?

She quoted the scripture softly to herself. "Though he slay me, yet will I trust in him."

It was true. One thousand coins could not buy God's favor, let alone a single coin. So what difference would it make? It was the right thing to do, and she believed it so. She reached out and dropped the coin into the receptacle. The sound of the one coin rolling down the metal tube and landing at the bottom on the many coins was loud enough for all to hear. Still she kept her head high, turned, and walked away.

Once off the temple grounds, she melted into the crowd in the streets. Suddenly, she felt a hand rest on her shoulder. She turned to face a small old woman, even older than she, dressed in fine clothes.

"What is your name, my daughter?" the woman asked.

"My name is Mary. Why do you ask?"

"The Master commented on your wonderful sacrifice," said the woman, smiling.

"It was no great sacrifice. It was just one coin," Mary responded.

"That's where you are wrong," said the woman. "The Master knew it was your last coin. He praised your faith and generosity."

"You keep saying, 'the Master'. You are too finely dressed to be a slave and have a master."

The old woman's eyes sparkled with delight. "I'm a very wealthy woman by the world's standards, though I was poor in spirit. But now I'm rich. Now I am a slave, and I have a master. His name is Jesus of Nazareth."

"I've heard of Him," Mary said. "Isn't He the young prophet?"

"I believe Him to be more than just a prophet." The old woman took hold of Mary's arm. "What will you do now that you have no money? Do you have a place to stay?"

"I live in the streets," Mary replied. "I will get by. I always have."

"My name is Odeleya. Allow me to help you."

"Thank you, but I cannot accept charity."

"Charity is not the only way to help. Can you cook?"

"I fed and raised three children after my husband died."

"You have three children; where are they now?"

"I haven't seen or heard from them in years. I don't even know if they are alive or if they care if I am."

The sadness of Mary's statement washed the smile from Odeleya's face. She waited till the awkward moment passed. "I've recently lost my cook. I live close by. If you can cook, you can work for me. The pay is nominal, but you will have food and shelter."

For the first time, Mary warmed up to the old woman. "I will not disappoint you, my mistress."

"You must call me Odeleya."

Now both women were smiling.

***

Mary proved true to her word. She knew her way around a kitchen like a fine craftsman and ran it like the captain of a seaworthy vessel. That first night, Odeleya told her to prepare enough for eight people.

First, Odeleya and her family...her son, Amir, and her daughter, Dana...were to be served. What was left was for Mary and the other servants.

One of the food servers entered the kitchen. "The mistress of the house wishes to see you."

Without hesitation, Mary wiped her hands and entered the dining quarters.

Odeleya, seated with her two children, smiled up at Mary. "Mary, let me congratulate you. That was a simply wonderful dinner."

"Thank you, Odeleya; I'm glad you liked it."

"What did you just say?" Amir barked up at Mary. "Did you just call my mother by her name?"

"Amir, I gave her permission to do so," Odeleya answered back.

"Well, don't let her do it in front of me," Amir demanded. He looked up at Mary. "From now on, you address my mother as Mistress. Do you understand?"

Mary looked to Dana, but her harsh look confirmed that she agreed with her brother. "Yes, I understand," Mary said as she turned to go back to the kitchen.

"Mother, since you began following this Jesus, you've lost your mind," said Dana. Amir grunted in approval of the statement.

"Perhaps, but I've found my soul," Odeleya countered. "It would be best if both of you went to listen to this Jesus."

"He's an upstart and a troublemaker," said Amir.

"My own children are heartless."

"How can you say that?" replied Amir. "We keep within the law, and we know our place."

"Which is what you should do," added Dana.

Odeleya rose and entered the kitchen. She found Mary cleaning up. "You must forgive my children. They have much to learn."

Mary placed the towel she was holding on the cutting board. 'Mistress..."

"Don't call me that!" Odeleya insisted.

Mary waited a moment and then took a deep breath. "Odeleya, I appreciate what you're doing for me; but why are you being so good to me?"

"Because God loves you, and I love God. So whatever God loves, I love."

"I don't understand," Mary said.

"That is why you should come with me to listen to Jesus. Then you will understand."

"I could never do that," Mary answered. "I've sinned all my life. I am not worthy."

"That is the beauty of what the Master offers. No one is worthy. But because He loves us, He is willing to forgive." Odeleya realized Mary was not ready. "One day you will hear His voice, you will be drawn to Him, and your life will never be the same. I will pray for that day, Mary."

The two women hugged as sisters.

***

The next few months were some of the most pleasant of Mary's life. She was happy in her work. She and Odeleya became close. Often, Odeleya would go to hear Jesus speak when He was in the area. She would return and tell Mary everything she heard. The good news of the gospel moved Mary's heart. Still, she was not ready to go to the Master and make a commitment. Odeleya kept Mary in her prayers.

One day, when Mary returned from a full day of shopping at the market, she passed the family physician as she entered the home. In the kitchen she was met by Amir and Dana.

"Our mother is on her deathbed. She is not expected to see out the day," Amir announced. "I am the master of this house. And I want you out of it, immediately."

Dana stood silently next to her brother, to support his commands. He continued. "I don't want you to take anything, because nothing here is yours. Now just turn around and leave."

"Please, let me say goodbye to your mother. I beg you," Mary pleaded.

There was a long moment of silence, and then Dana spoke, "Let her. What harm could it do?"

"Very well," said Amir. "You may have one minute to say goodbye."

Mary rushed to Odeleya's room. She found the old woman on her bed, weak and dying. She looked up at Mary through half-closed eyes.

"Don't look so sad, Mary. I am going to a better place."

"You mustn't die," Mary begged.

"I'm not afraid," Odeleya said. "But I am afraid for you. Go, find the Master. Find Jesus, before it's too late." She reached under her pillow and brought forth a small sack. "Knowing my son, he will not let you leave with a coin to your name. Here, take this. It isn't much, but you can hide it within your robe."

Mary did as she was told and hid the sack in her large sleeve. Just then, Amir and Dana entered.

"Time is up," he announced, "time for you to leave."

Mary took hold of Odeleya's hand. "I love you."

"I love you, too, my sister," Odeleya said. "Now, go; and God be with you."

***

Mary walked the streets in a daze, hardly aware of her surroundings. Her heart felt as if it were breaking. She'd forgotten about the sack till its contents pressed hard against her arm. She took it out of her sleeve. She reached in and pulled out a small, white alabaster jar. She took off the stopper and put it to her nose. She was familiar with the scent. It was Nard…the breathtaking and pricey perfumed ointment. On the market it could be sold for a year's wages.

The day was still hot, and many of the homes had their windows and doors open to let in what little breeze there was. As she passed one home, she heard Him. It was like the voice of an old friend. She couldn't make out the words, but it called out to her. She stopped at the doorway of the home it came from and looked in. There seated on the floor at the head of a table was Jesus. How did she know it was Jesus? She had never seen or heard Him before. Still, something in her heart knew it was Him.

She entered, walked to Jesus, and fell at his feet. "Oh, Master, forgive me, a miserable sinner."

He placed his hand on her head. "My daughter, your faith has saved you. Your sins are forgiven."

The sound of men grumbling filled the air. "Only God can forgive sins," many in the room shouted.

Mary reached into her sack and took out the alabaster jar. She removed the stopper. Immediately, the scent of the perfume filled the room. She began to pour it over Jesus' feet and then on the crown of his head. Many men, including some of the apostles shouted their disagreement. "Such a waste! That could have been sold, and the money used to help the poor!"

"The poor you will always have, but you will not always have Me," Jesus said. "This woman has done what she could and has anointed My body for burial."

Mary's tears poured from her eyes onto the Master's feet, which she dried with her hair. She rose and bowed.

"Go in peace, My daughter, and sin no more," Jesus said.

Mary slowly backed away.

"Wait, My child; you have forgotten your sack," Jesus said, holding it to her.

She took the sack and walked backwards out of the house, bowing and giving praise. Outside, she went to put the sack into her pocket, when she felt something hard and heavy. There had been something else besides the jar within it. She shook it; it jingled like hundreds of tiny bells. She opened it and looked inside. There at the bottom of the sack were dozens of silver and gold coins, enough for her to live out her life in comfort.

With tears in her eyes, she marched to the temple. It was time to make another offering to God.

THE END

30

CONSPIRACY

In the upper room, where only the night before the apostles gathered for the Passover feast, they assembled again on the night of the Sabbath. They sat at the same table, ate the same food…only this night, their world was different.

"I hope none of you mind me sitting at the head of the table. But one of us has to take charge, and I figure it might as well be me," Peter announced.

Either no one cared, or no one felt like arguing, but they remained silent.

"Good," continued Peter. "Then let's get down to business. I'm sure all of you agree things have changed in the past twenty-four hours and need addressing. First off, apostle-wise, we're one short since Judas Iscariot is no longer with us. His passing leaves two openings that need filling. Judas was the treasurer. A bad one, I must admit; but he's gone, and we need to elect a new treasurer. I nominate Matthew. I mean, he used to be a tax collector. I'd say he's our best choice. All those in favor say 'Aye'." He paused for a response. "All those against Matthew being treasurer say 'Nay'." Silence, the 'Ayes' have it."

Matthew stood up and took a bow. "I'd like thank everyone for their vote of confidence. I won't let you down. I'll handle the money like it was my own."

"That's what we're afraid of," said Simon the Zealot. Everyone laughed.

"All right, all right, calm down," said Peter. "The next piece of business is that we're one apostle short, and twelve is such a nice round number. That's why I've invited my old friend, Benny the Benjamite. Stand up, Benny; and let the fellas take a look at you."

Benny stood and smiled. "I appreciate Pete asking me here tonight. I really don't know if I want the job. I'd like to hear what it's all about before I decide."

"Oh, you're just going to love it, I promise you," said John.

"Just think of it. You'll be part of the beginning of one of the greatest religions in the world," said Bartholomew.

"Yeah, and with just twelve of us, think of all the room for advancement," added Phillip.

"I'll believe it when I see it," grumbled Thomas.

"Sit down, Benny," said Peter. "Why don't all of us help Benny decide by letting him in on our plans for the future?"

Thaddeus leaned across the table to address Benny. "As you know, we were all followers of Jesus of Nazareth. He was a real nice guy; you would have liked him. Anyways, we followed him around for three years, building up this new religion. He was a good talker, very persuasive. By the end of three years, we had a slew of followers all over: north, south, east and west. And just when we thought it was smooth sailing, Jesus gets arrested. They hit him with the book. Then they got the Romans to agree to have him executed. Now we're on our own."

"So what are you going to do?" Benny asked.

Andrew jumped in at this point. "Pete, here, has it all planned out." He turned to his brother. "Tell him, Pete."

"Well, I don't like to brag; but I think it's a pretty good plan," said Peter. "Early tomorrow morning, before the sun comes up, we go down to Jesus' tomb. Roll the rock away from the tomb, take the body, and hide it."

"Why would you do that?" asked Benny.

"We'll spread rumors that he raised from the dead. The people will eat it up. Great religions are built on such myths. And we'll be the head of it."

"That's a great idea," said Benny. "Think of all the money we can make."

"Oh, there won't be any money," replied Peter. "I've figured it every which way, and we come up penniless."

"Then power," said Benny. "We'll have great power."

"I don't think so," continued Peter. "As I figure it, most people will hate us and try to kill us." Peter rolled out a map on the table in front of Benny. "This is a map of the known world. We'll all head in different directions, spreading the news of our new religion."

"I don't know about that," said Benny. "My wife doesn't like to travel, and we've got two kids."

"Oh, there won't be any wives or children," James, son of Zebedee declared. "Most of the time, you'll be alone and on foot. You'll be cold, hungry, and tired, hiking for days from one city to the next. You'll sleep out in the elements and catch all sorts of diseases. When you come to a new town or village, you start preaching. Hopefully, all they'll do is run you out of town. Of course, there is always the possibility they'll imprison you for your faith. You may spend years locked away in a cold cell, starving to death."

"And let's not forget torture," said Philip. "Flogging is a favorite with both Jews and Gentiles. Dismemberment is popular lately, and so is the rack. I only hope that when they torture me that I have the strength to not break down and admit our religion is a sham."

"Wait, let me get this straight," said Benny. "You want me to join your little group and help you steal a dead body to spread a myth that our leader is risen and alive. Then we go preach this religion all over the world. And not only do we not see any profit for our efforts, we may suffer for our actions. I don't get it. What's the upside to all this?"

"You'll be part of starting the largest religion of all time. Think of it, you're children and your children's children will live in a world with a religion that you helped start. Even though you probably won't live to see it, I think it's a grand and noble gesture."

"Grand and noble? It's a made-up religion based on trickery!" shouted Benny. "A man can get killed doing this kind of work!"

"I don't doubt it," said Thomas. "I'm sure we'll all suffer for the cause at some point, even to the death. It wouldn't surprise me if all of us wind up dead in a few years in some faraway and remote part of the world, alone and penniless.

And not just any old death, but some real nasty deaths like torture, beheadings, stabbings, and, dare I say it, crucifixions, or worse."

"I can't think of anything worse," added Peter.

"You talk about all of us dying like it's a good thing," said Benny.

"It is a good thing," Thomas replied.

"How's that good?"

"It's good because it gives validity to our story. When they see us dying for the cause, they'll believe it and become followers. If I can agree with my brother Phillip, I only hope that when they're going to kill me in some horrific way, I don't break down and admit that we stole the body and it's all a big hoax to try to save my life."

"You guys are all nuts," said Benny. "Don't you see? Don't you get it? Why would you die for a lie?"

"Hey, that rhymes! Die…lie…you're a poet, and you didn't even know it," John said, and everyone laughed.

Benny looked about him and realized he would never get his point across; it was hopeless. Suddenly, he slapped his forehead. "What am I thinking? Today is Saturday. I promised the wife I'd be home for dinner. Listen, I really had a swell time, but I gotta go." He literally ran for the door.

"So when will you give us your decision?" Peter called out.

"I'll call you," said Benny over his shoulder as he dashed out the door.

THE END

31

DIVINE WIND

Katsu stood on the runway watching the ground crew load his single-propeller Mitsubishi with explosives. When they finished and no one was around, he climbed the ladder up to the cockpit. He pulled the pilot's seat forward, and placed in a few items, and then replaced the seat. Stepping down and away from the ladder, he looked around. He'd finished just in time; the others were coming.

A small band played military music. He and two other pilots stood before a long table; behind it were three officers. The commanding officer raised his hand, and the band stopped. He praised the three pilots for their bravery and sacrifice. He reminded them of the Bushido Code: loyalty and honor until death. To be a Kamikaze pilot is the noblest rank in the Japanese Air Force. He was proud of them. He saluted them with tears in his eyes. He led everyone in the cry, *Tennouheika Banzai! Banzai! Banzai!*...Ten thousand years of life for the Emperor!

One of the officers poured sake into three cups and offered them to the pilots. Katsu looked into his glass. Normally, rice wine is clear; this was dark...laced with opium. They held up their cups in a toast and downed their drinks in quick gulps. Katsu poured his drink down his chin, the liquid landing on the front of his jacket. In the excitement, it went unnoticed. He'd gotten away with it.

After much saluting and fanfare, he and the other pilots walked to their planes, climbed the ladders, and got in the cockpits. This would be the hard part. One of the ground crew got up on his ladder. He held a chain and shackles. It was Kamikaze tradition to chain the pilot in.

"Why do you disgrace me like this?" Katsu asked the man.

"Disgrace you?" the man replied. "But this is a hero's death. It is an honorable way to die."

"No, you dishonor me by chaining me in. I have made a vow to die for my country and the Emperor. I swear on the souls of my ancestors I will do my duty. You are taking my freewill to do so. Please, do not disgrace me."

Katsu's plea touched the man's heart. In tears, the man let the chain fall to the floor of the cockpit. He sealed Katsu in, descended, and removed the ladder. They started their engines. With one last salute from the commanding officer, they taxied down the runway.

The three planes flew in tight formation out over the ocean. Katsu made sure he flew on the outside of the group. Up ahead, an American destroyer was on the horizon. Katsu thought of flying off, but he feared the other two would try to shoot him down for desertion. He'd wait till they were close to the destroyer, and the other two would be busy with the mission.

When they were in firing distance, the destroyer began shooting at them. Katsu banked his plane and started a dive toward the ocean below. He thought of stalling his engine to make the other two pilots believe he was hit by enemy fire. But why bother? So they would curse him with their last breath. What did it matter? They'd be dead in the next moment, and he'd be alive.

He brought the plane down slowly, cruising a few feet above the water. When the belly of the plane hit, it spun on the surface of the water like a child's top. As he wheeled around, he saw the other two planes crash into the destroyer. The explosions were like two little black and red mushroom clouds.

His propeller stopped spinning. He had safely landed. The plane would only float for so long; he had to act fast. Opening the hatch, he took off his safety belt. Standing, he pulled his seat forward. He took out the inflatable raft, pulled the cord, threw it in the water, and watched it grow to a four-man raft. He took a knapsack filled with rice balls and dried fish and slung it over his shoulder. There was a large canteen of fresh water that he hung on his other shoulder. With one mighty leap, he was in the raft. He used a small wooden paddle to move from the plane that was sinking fast.

When he was a safe distance from the plane, off on the horizon the destroyer exploded. The sound was deafening and shook the air around him. He could feel the heat of the flames and black smoke shot up to the clouds. He leaned back in the raft and watched. He watched for a long time. It seemed as if the fire would never go out when suddenly, the ship sank in less than a minute. The sea was calm again.

After Katsu drifted for a time, he heard the voice of someone crying out in the distance. He took his paddle and rowed toward it. It was an American sailor...surely, a survivor of the sunken ship...struggling to stay afloat.

"Here, take my hand," Katsu said. They locked hands, and Katsu pulled him on board. It took some time for the sailor to regain his breath.

"You speak English," said the man, looking at Katsu.

"Four years at the University of Chicago," Katsu replied.

"Oh, great," the sailor laughed. "I'm stuck in the middle of the ocean on a life raft with a Cub's fan."

"Actually, I always felt partial to the Yankees; but I never mentioned it on campus."

"The name's Jack. What's yours?"

"My name's Katsu."

The sailor got his breath back. "So, Katsu, what do we do now?"

"Well, technically, Jack, you are on Japanese territory. That would make you my prisoner."

Jack laughed. "Well, you won't have to worry about me trying to escape. Do we have any food?"

Katsu held up his knapsack. "We've got enough food and water for ten days, if we ration it out slowly."

"If you had any sense," Jack said, "you'd toss me overboard."

"If I had any sense," Katsu said, "I never would have taken you on. Whatever...we can play Twenty Questions tomorrow. Let's get some sleep."

Jack didn't need persuading. He closed his eyes, and that's all it took. Katsu lay on his side, placed his head on his knapsack, and shut his eyes.

***

The next morning, Katsu gave one half of a rice ball and a morsel of dried fish to Jack and took the same amount for himself as well. They ate slowly. When they finished, they each took one swallow of water.

"So what's the plan?" Jack asked.

Katsu pointed east. "Fifty miles in that direction is land."

"Piece of cake," replied Jack.

"So, Jack, where you from?"

"No place that you ever heard of. Stowe, Vermont."

"Sure, I know it. Great ski country."

"You've been there?"

"Once. I went with some school chums on winter break."

"Wow, it's a small world."

"Not really," Katsu said. "Not when all you have is one paddle. I'll take the first shift rowing."

***

They took turns rowing. By night fall, they were exhausted. They decided they'd try to go without food or drink till the morning. Again it wasn't difficult to fall asleep.

Late at night, they were awakened by crashing thunder and bright flashes of lightening. The rain started. They did their best to keep the tiny raft from filling up with water. The waves grew till they were as tall as a building, and washed over the raft. The sea tossed the raft about. In the confusion, the knapsack of food and the canteen of water were washed overboard. It wasn't until morning that the rain stopped and the sea calmed. Dog-tired, they fell asleep.

They woke midday. The scorching sun overhead burned their skin. Jack dipped his hand in the ocean and tried to cool his face. He opened the front of his shirt, exposing his dog tags and a cross.

"So, you're a Christian?" Katsu asked.

"I sure am, and proud of it. What are you?" Jack asked.

"A bad Buddhist, if there is such a thing. I never thought much of religion."

"Well, that's great," Jack said. "It seems God put us together for a reason: for me to evangelize you."

Katsu laughed. "Are you saying God made me a Kamikaze pilot, let us blow up a ship with thousands of sailors, and set us adrift together in the middle of the ocean just so you can save my soul?"

"I couldn't say for sure," Jack said. "His ways are not our ways. But I tell ya, I wouldn't put it past Him."

"Well, we've got no food and water. All we have is time so I might as well be amused by your fairytale," Katsu said.

"Oh, it's not a fairytale," Jack said, pulling out a miniature Bible from his top pocket. "It's factual and very scientific."

"Scientific?" Katsu questioned.

"Sure, like this." Jack opened to the first page and moved his finger over the words as he read. "In the beginning, God created the heavens and the earth. That means God created time, space, and matter. 'In the beginning' is time. 'Heaven' is space, and 'Earth' is matter."

"Interesting," Katsu said. "Go ahead; I'm listening."

Jack continued reading the entire day, explaining each passage as well as he could. He read till they fell asleep. In the morning, Jack continued where he left off. It was clear the reading was a strain on Jack, having nothing to eat or drink.

"You don't have to do this, you know," Katsu said.

"That's where you're wrong," Jack said. "We may not get out of this alive. I can't make you accept Jesus as your Savior. But if it's the last thing I do, I refuse to leave this body till you hear the full Gospel."

Katsu didn't have the strength to argue, so he leaned back and listened.

Days went by. In their failing strength, they couldn't remember how many. Jack's voice became weaker. His parched throat hurt as he spoke; still he continued. Finally, in the middle of second Corinthians, Katsu stopped him.

"Enough, you've done your job well. I see and understand it all now. I want to accept Jesus Christ as my savior," Katsu said.

Jack led him through the Sinner's Prayer.

"I want to make it complete," Katsu said. "I want to be baptized."

"Well, we have enough water," Jack said in a tired and gruff voice.

Slowly, Katsu rolled out of the raft and into the water. Jack placed his hand on Katsu's head. "Do you accepted Jesus Christ as your Lord and Savior?" Jack asked.

Katsu was quick to respond. "I do."

"I baptize you in the name of the Father, the Son, and the Holy Spirit." Jack gently pushed Katsu's head underwater. Once he bobbed up, Katsu, with Jack's help, got back into the raft. Normally, getting out and back in would have been a simple act. But in their weakened state, it was an ordeal. They both fell into a deep unconsciousness.

***

When Katsu regained consciousness, he could barely open his eyes. He was aware of voices around him. Through barely opened eyes, he saw American sailors carrying Jack up and out of the raft. He felt hands taking hold of him and lifting him up also. They were being saved. Again, Katsu went out cold.

Katsu woke in a bed, clearly in the medical facility of an American destroyer. There were doctors and naval officers around him.

"*Onamae wa nandesuka?*" said one of the younger officers.

"My name is Katsu. And your Japanese is atrocious."

"So you speak English," said what Katsu believed to be the senior officer.

"I spent sometime in the States before the war," Katsu said.

"What was your mission?" asked the officer.

"I was a pilot with a Kamikaze squad. I was on a mission with two other planes to crash into an American destroyer, nearly two weeks ago."

"Sounds like the USS Emmons off Okinawa, sir," said one of the petty officers.

"I don't know the name of it," Katsu said. "But I can give you a location, if you show me a map."

"How is it you didn't crash into the destroyer?" asked the senior officer.

"I decided I didn't want to die for a lost cause," Katsu replied.

"And how is that you were found with an American sailor on your raft?"

"After the ship sank, I found him swimming around. I didn't have the heart to leave him stranded in the middle of the ocean."

"That's a strange attitude for an enemy to take," one of the officers mentioned.

"I suppose I never considered us as enemies," Katsu responded. He turned to one of the doctors. "How long have I been out?"

"We picked you up three days ago,"

"How's Jack?" Katsu asked.

"Jack? Oh, you mean the American sailor in the raft with you. We had a burial at sea the second day after we found you."

Katsu looked mournful, nearly in tears. "I'm sorry to hear that. He was my brother."

"How is that?"

"I said...oh, never mind. I can't explain it."

"That brings us to another point," said the senior officer. "We thank you and feel it was a noble gesture to bring the body with you. But why did you keep it on board?"

"He said he refused to leave his body till I'd heard the gospel," Katsu said.

One of the doctors spoke up. "You must have been out of your head with heat and hunger. I examined the body. It was severely damage by the blast. He was dead when you pulled him from the water."

Katsu hesitated and then whispered, "His ways are not our ways."

"How is that?" asked the senior officer.

"I was just thinking about God," Katsu said. "His ways are not our ways, and I wouldn't put anything past Him."

THE END

32

REASSIGNMENT THERAPY

The waiting room was empty save for the Chalfon family. Mrs. Chalfon spent her time reading with her nose in the fashion magazines. Mr. Chalfon sat mentally assessing and calculating the price of the furniture in the room and the artwork on the walls. Doctor Lieberman was said to be one of the finest psychiatrist in the city and certainly one of the most expensive. At two hundred a session, Mr. Chalfon wondered how many sessions it would take. Then he felt guilty for thinking such thoughts. How could he put a price on his son's well-being and happiness? Their son, Todd, was a tall slender, young man of sixteen. His dark good looks were a combination of all of his parents' attractive qualities. He stood reading the diplomas that covered the far wall.

"Gee, this Doctor Lieberman must be one smart guy," Todd remarked.

"At these prices, he better be," said his father.

Mrs. Chalfon shot a cold look at her husband that would have killed any ordinary man who hadn't over many long years built up a resistance to such venom.

A door at the other end of the room opened, and a smiling young woman stepped in. "The doctor's ready to see you now." The Chalfon family marched into the next room. The smiling woman closed the door behind them.

Doctor Lieberman's office smelled of old books and furniture polish. Lieberman rose from behind his desk and shook each of their hands. "My name is Doctor Lieberman. Pleased to meet you; please sit down." He returned to his seat as well. Placing his folded hands on his desk and with a serious but friendly tone, he spoke directly. "So, tell me, what seems to be the matter?"

Both Todd and his father remained silent. They always left matters needing explanation to Mrs. Chalfon. "It's Todd, our son. He's a good boy and smart, too…very popular with all the other children at school. But lately he's been depressed, maybe suicidal."

"What are you depressed about?" Lieberman asked looking at the young man.

Before Todd could speak, his mother continued. "It's his identity, doctor."

"His identity? What's wrong with his identity?"

"I mean, he knows who he is; he knows he's Todd," maintained Mrs. Chalfon. "It's his sexual identity, if you catch my drift, doctor."

"I'm sorry, Mrs. Chalfon. I don't catch your drift."

"He's not happy with his sexual identity. He needs…" Mrs. Chalfon searched for the word. "What do they call it? Oh, yes, he needs sexual identity reassignment therapy. He wants to change his sexual identity…what he's attracted to, if you know what I mean."

Lieberman looked at young Todd and then to his mother. "Mrs. Chalfon, I'm sorry; but sexual identity reassignment therapy has been outlawed in this state."

"What do you mean? Why can't he be allowed to change his sexual identity, if he wants to? Especially since it's causing him so much pain and misery."

"Mrs. Chalfon, again, I'm sorry; but my hands are tied. If your son is homosexual, I'd be glad to work with him to accept who he is and become comfortable in his own skin, so to speak. But I'm afraid I can't make your son straight."

"Who said anything about making him straight?" Mrs. Chalfon huffed. "He's already straight. You can't stop him from chasing young girls. No, doctor, my son wants you to help him become gay."

Lieberman looked at Todd. "Is that true?" he asked with wide-eyed amazement.

"Yes, it is," replied Todd. "I'm tired of living this way. Something's got to change, or I don't know what I'll do."

"I don't understand," said Lieberman.

"What's to understand?" Todd continued. "Times have changed. Why would I want to live the boring life of a heterosexual? The tide has turned, and gay people are leading the pack. If I were gay, there'd be more opportunities for me. People would envy me. I could get a better job after college and make more money. Gay people enjoy life more. They dress better. They dance better. They look better. They live better. How many poor gay men do you know? Hollywood loves gays. Politicians love gays. The world loves gays. Why should I be condemned to a life lived on the outskirts of what's happening?"

"But your mother said you're attracted to women."

"I know that's a problem; but I'm sure I can get over such feelings."

"When did you realize you were attracted to girls?"

"I was so young, I don't remember. Now it only upsets me. I feel…" Todd thought for a moment. "I feel shame. That's what I feel, shame and frustration. I don't see anything in the future for me. Gay men have it all. And the women….women always like to hang out with gay men."

"Yes, but if you were truly homosexual, it wouldn't make any difference. You wouldn't be attracted to them. Don't you think?" Lieberman assumed

"Well," said Todd. "I don't think anyone could be *that* gay. Nothing in this world is a hundred percent."

"Excuse me, Doc," Mr. Chalfon muttered. "About how much do you thing this is going to cost?"

"I'm not sure I'm going to take the case, Mr. Chalfon," replied Lieberman.

Mrs. Chalfon slapped her husband on the arm. "How could you ask such a question? Your own flesh and blood son is suffering!"

"It's not that," said Mr. Chalfon. "I was just wondering if there's some kind of shortcut. Maybe there's a surgery or a drug or shock treatment? Something you could do in a day or so."

"Mr. Chalfon, psychoanalysis isn't a quick fix. It takes time."

"And money," added Mr. Chalfon.

Lieberman turned his attention back to Todd. "Tell me, Todd, what are your feelings towards men? Do you find yourself attracted to them?"

"Not in the least," said Todd. "But I'm working on it, and I've made some progress."

"Really?" said Lieberman. "What have you done?"

"Well, recently I broke off with my girlfriend."

"And how did that go?" Lieberman asked.

"Not too good at first. She was really angry with me. But when I told her why I did it, she forgave me and said she admired me for taking a stand. She said I was some kind of hero to her, and she wished she had the same courage to do the same. Then I told all my friends at school I was gay."

"How did that turn out?"

"They put my name in the running for Homecoming Queen. And I would have won, too, if it wasn't for Doug Tebel coming out first. But I came in a close second."

Lieberman looked to Todd's parents. "Does your family have any religious affiliation?"

Mr. Chalfon spoke up. "We used to, many years ago when Todd was little."

"Why did you stop?"

"The pastor refused to perform a wedding ceremony for a same-sex couple. The government came in, arrested the pastor, and closed the place down. After that, we figured, why bother?"

"Enough of this," said Mrs. Chalfon. "Will you help our son or not?"

Lieberman looked glum. "I'm afraid, Mrs. Chalfon, I'll have to pass. I don't feel good about it. I'd be glad to give you a few recommendations of doctors I'm sure would take the case."

Mrs. Chalfon rose, walked to the door, and opened it. Instinctively, her son and husband stood and walked out the door. The last thing Mrs. Chalfon said before she walked out and slammed the door was, "Doctor Lieberman, you will be hearing from our lawyer!"

Michael Edwin Q.

THE END

33

A FATHER'S LOVE

Rosaline tiptoed across the floor of the waiting room to Ms. Chaplin's office door. Her little, brown leather purse that always hung from her shoulder, she held in both hands so its contents wouldn't rattle and give her away. She was never without her purse that held the few possessions that she had in the world.

She leaned forward and peered through the keyhole. She saw Ms. Chaplin sitting behind her desk, speaking to a man and woman seated across from her. Rosaline couldn't see them for their backs were to the door. Not able to hear a word, she pressed her ear against the door.

"Well, Mr. and Mrs. Fairweather," Ms. Chaplin said, smiling with her hands folded on top of her desk, "what do you think? Will you consider adopting Rosaline?"

"I don't know," said Mrs. Fairweather. "I must say, she's not an attractive child. I mean, she doesn't look anything like either one of us."

"Beauty is in the eye of the beholder,'" Ms. Chaplin recited.

"So I've heard," said Mrs. Fairweather. "I just don't know."

"She's a little on the plump side," said Mr. Fairweather. "A bit too round for a seven-year-old, don't you think? Probably cost an arm and a leg to keep her feed."

"Rosaline does have a weight issue," Ms. Chaplin admitted. "Most of her problem is that she gets so little exercise, being in such poor health from birth."

"That's another thing," complained Mr. Fairweather. "What are you trying to put over on us, Ms. Chaplin?"

Ms. Chaplin lost her smile and unfolded her hands. "I don't know what you mean, Mr. Fairweather."

"Come now, Ms. Chaplin; I understand what you're doing," said Mr. Fairweather. "I don't blame you. I suppose you have to present the least attractive children first, in hopes you can find them a home, before you show the real winners."

"I don't know what you're talking about," Ms. Chaplin said through clenched teeth.

"Don't play games with me, Ms. Chaplin. You're trying to pawn off this...this ugly, fat, sickly seven-year-old on us."

"And looking at her grades, I wouldn't call her smart, either," added Mrs. Fairweather.

"Why don't you stop wasting your time and ours, Ms. Chaplin," said Mr. Fairweather, "and show us some of the higher quality kids you've got here."

Ms. Chaplin jumped to her feet. "These are children, Mr. Fairweather, not cattle. Rosaline is a beautiful, sweet, loving child; and you don't deserve to have her or any other child. I only pray that someday you both change; and until that day I hope you never get your hands on a child. There is nothing for you here; so kindly, please leave."

Mr. and Mrs. Fairweather rose from their seats, huffing inaudible words under their breaths. They made for the office door. When the doorknob turned, Rosaline ran across the room and landed in her chair. Mr. and Mrs. Fairweather marched out of the waiting room. Feeling too uncomfortable to look into their faces, she stared at her feet dangling a foot from the floor.

A moment later, Ms. Chaplin exited her office. She smiled at Rosaline as she walked to her.

"Now, how long have you been out here?" Ms. Chaplin asked.

"Long enough to hear everything," Rosaline said, still looking down.

Ms. Chaplin put a curved finger under the girl's chin and gently lifted her head until they were looking eye to eye. "Listen, those people weren't very nice. You shouldn't believe anything they said. You're a beautiful little girl. You're smart, and you're worth loving."

"Yeah, but I'm still an orphan."

"Not for long, I promise you," Ms. Chaplin said with true sincerity. "You're a good kid. There's someone out there who'll love you like there's no tomorrow. You'll see."

"Yeah, I guess so," Rosaline said, sounding down-and-out. "May I please be excused?"

"Of course you may. Go outside and get some air. You'll feel better. Just remember..."

"Don't play too hard. Yeah, I know. I shouldn't get too overheated."

Ms. Chaplin bent low, hugged the child and gave her a kiss on her cheek. It didn't seem to matter much to Rosaline at the moment. Ms. Chaplin stood listening to Rosaline's footsteps going down the hall and the rattle of her treasures in her purse.

***

Outside, Rosaline heard the other children in the playground behind the building. She was in no mood to see them and have to explain what happened. She started down the walkway lined with trees and wooden benches. Up ahead, she saw a man seated on one of the benches. As she got closer, she felt a little afraid. She didn't recognize him. He had long hair and a beard; and his clothing was strange, nothing like she'd ever seen before. When she came up to him, she decided she was not going to be afraid. She stopped directly in front of him.

"Hello," she said timidly.

"Hello, Rosaline," the man said.

"Say. How do you know my name?"

"I know many things," he said.

"What's your name?"

"I go by many names; but you can call me Joshua."

"What are you doing here?"

"I've been waiting for you, Rosaline."

"You've been waiting for me? Why?"

"I thought you might need a friend just now."

"Thanks, but I've got plenty of friends. What I need is a family. Do you have a family?"

"Yes I do…a very big family."

"You see, I'm an orphan," Rosaline said sadly. "I wish someone would adopt me. I wish I had a family."

Joshua moved over and pointed to the space next to him as an invitation for her to sit, which she did. "Well, I'll tell you. If you'd like, I could ask my father to adopt you."

"You just said you have a big family. I don't think your father would want any more family."

"That's not so," Joshua said. "He's always telling me we have to add members to the family. A family can never be too big."

"Gee, you think he'd really like me?"

"I'm positive. A beautiful, smart young woman such as you…why the family wouldn't be complete without you. Only, there is one thing."

"I knew there'd be a catch," Rosaline pouted.

"You have to be a perfectly good little girl," Joshua stated firmly.

A smile came to Rosaline's face. "That's fine; I'm pretty good, as kids go."

"Really?" Joshua said, sounding inquisitive. "Have you ever lied?"

"Not too often," Rosaline said, "and never really any bad lies."

"Then you have lied?"

Rosaline reluctantly nodded.

"Have you ever stolen anything?" Joshua continued.

"Nothing very big, maybe a cookie."

"And have you ever been angry?" Joshua asked.

"Sheila Mae sleeps in the bed next to mine. She makes an awful racket when she sleeps. I have to hit her with a pillow to get her to stop. I mean, I don't hate her or anything like that; but she sure makes me angry."

Still smiling, he shook his head. "Ah, Rosaline, I know you so want to be a good girl; but that does not sound like perfection to me; and my father wants you to be perfect. What you've done, your actions, are what we call sin. Do you know what sin is?"

Rosaline nodded, "I think I do."

He continued, "There is a penalty for sin, you know?"

"I'll gladly pay it if I can be part of your family," Rosaline pleaded.

"Oh, no, Rosaline, you don't know what you're asking. The price is too great." Joshua smiled and held up on finger. "But there is a way. You can let me pay the price for your sins."

"No," Rosaline begged him, "I couldn't let you do that."

"It's too late," Joshua said. "It's already done. All that's left is for you to admit you've done wrong, promise never to repeat them, and accept the sacrifice I've made in your name. Besides, it will be my first act as your new big brother."

"You would be my big brother?"

"It would be my honor," Joshua said.

"Then I do," Rosaline said. "I promise to always be a good girl and to accept your sacrifice and you as my big brother."

Joshua's smile grew big as his eyes grew softer. "Welcome to the family, Rosaline." He reached over and hugged her.

"So when do I meet my new family, and when do I see my new Dada." Rosaline asked.

"In a short time," Joshua replied.

"But I need to see him now."

"Would that make you happy?"

"Oh, yes, very much."

He pulled her close to him, held her tightly, and, with one hand, stroked her hair. "Now close your eyes, little sister. We're going home to see Dada."

***

Even in plainclothes, as he entered Ms. Chaplin's office, she knew him to be a police officer.

"My name is Sergeant Kendrick. I'm sorry to bother you at a time like this, Ms. Chaplin; but there are some formalities. The ambulance has just left. There'll be an autopsy, but it's just procedure. The paramedics said it looked like natural causes."

"Rosaline was always a sickly child. She had a weak heart," Ms. Chaplin responded.

"Then why was she playing with the other children?" he asked.

"Oh, she wasn't playing. One of the teachers found her lying on one of the benches on campus."

Sergeant Kendrick held out Rosaline's tiny purse to her. "I figured you'd want to have this. It's filled with what you'd expect a seven-year-old to treasure. Some coins, a thimble, lipstick and nail polish, and a few family pictures. But we also found something else that we can't explain. Maybe you can?"

Ms. Chaplin took a folded piece of paper from Sergeant Kendrick. She opened it and read it slowly and carefully.

"I don't understand," Ms. Chaplin said. "Is this some kind of joke? This is a certificate of adoption. It has Rosaline's name on it, and the date is today!"

"Could the child have typed it?" Kendrick asked.

"Sergeant, she was only seven years old. She could hardly spell, let alone type."

Kendrick pointed to the bottom of the page. "And whose signature is this? Who is…Joshua?"

THE END

34

WILLY AND SPLINTERS

The club Zanzibar was smokier than usual. The crowd was drunker and louder than usual. Still, though the audience ignored them, Willy Mecum continued his act. He sat on stage in a hot, white spotlight with his dummy, Splinters, on his lap. Ventriloquism is difficult enough without people ignoring you, and jokes aren't funny if nobody hears them. But still, it was a living; and the club needed something to fill in the time between dancers.

Willy was a tired-looking little man who appeared older than forty, which he was. Years of performing at lodge meetings, children's parties, stag parties, and nightclubs had taken their toll.

Splinters, on the other hand, still looked like a twelve-year-old boy with his dark, wavy hair; his bright smile with moving lips; eyes that rolled around and around; and eyebrows that bounce up and down. Whenever they hit the stage, there was always a woman or two who yelled, "He's so cute!" Lacquered wood and paint take longer to yellow and age than flesh and blood.

Even with loud Boom-boom-crash from the drummer in the band after every joke, it seemed like a long, uphill struggle for Willy and Splinters.

"Say, Willy, what do you call a chicken crossing the road?"

"I don't know, Splinters. What do you call a chicken crossing the road?"

"Poultry in motion."

Boom-boom-crash, nothing.

A drunk stood up and shouted, "Hey, get off the stage."

Splinters turned to look at the drunk; his eyebrows went up and down as he spoke. "All the world is but a stage', my friend.

Only you got a bit part; a nonspeaking part, pal. So why don't you button it and sit down."

"Your momma!" the drunk yelled back laughing.

Splinters leaned forward, his neck stretching to twice its length. "Listen, buddy, my mother was a mighty oak, my father was a sequoia, and all my brothers and sisters are baseball bats. So you don't wanna mess with my family, chum."

"Leave him alone," said the woman at the drunk's table. "I think he's cute."

"I just hate bein' told off by a piece of wood," said the drunk, sitting back down.

Splinter broke into song. The band backed him up. "If it's wood, it's good. If it's good, it's wood. Give me a W. Give me a double O. Give me a D. What's that spell? Wood, wood, yea, wood!"

Somehow, Willy and Splinters got through the last five minutes of their act. The audience came alive as the next dancer hit the stage to whistles and jeers.

In their dressing room, Willy placed Splinters on the couch and sat in front of his mirror and began to remove his makeup. He could see Splinters' image in the mirror. The dummy smiled and winked at him.

"Don't try to make up with me," said Willy. "That cutesy stuff don't work on me anymore."

"What's the matter, Willy? You angry with me?"

"I'm not angry, Splinters; I'm just tired of you saying whatever comes into that wooden head of yours. They think I'm the one talking, not you. An irritated customer isn't going to hit you. I'm the one who gets the black eye."

"I'm sorry, Willy. I can't help it. You know how I am. I've always got to tell the truth, even if it hurts."

"Yeah, but I'm the one who gets the hurt," Willy replied.

"You know what they say," said Splinters, "honesty is the best policy'."

"The only policy I'm going to need is an insurance policy, if you don't stop mouthing off."

"Sorry, Willy; I'll try my best."

"Well, see that you do," Willy said gently. "Listen, we're here for the rest of week; but we're low on funds. I'm going to ask the owner if I can get an advance till payday. I won't be long. You stay here and try not to get into any trouble."

Willy left the room, closing the door behind him. Splinters sat motionless on the couch, eyeing himself in the mirror.

A minute later, the door opened; and two showgirls poked their heads into the room. They were both tall and were made taller by high heels. They wore their hair piled high and arrayed with ostrich feathers.

"I tell ya, the little guy can talk even when Willy ain't around," said one of the dancers.

"You blondes are all alike. The bleach's been seeping into your skull. You got a screw loose somewhere," said the other.

Splinters turned his head to them; his eyebrows went up. "I agree. Whoever heard of a dummy talking on his own? The girl must have sawdust for brains."

"See, I told ya he could talk," said the first girl.

"It must be some kind of trick," said the second.

"Does your mother know you do this?" Splinters asked.

They both laughed. "I think he's cute," said the first.

"Does your mother know you're not married; and you been living with some guy for the past six months?"

"Well, I never..." said the first girl.

"That's your problem," said Splinter. "You'd be better off if you didn't. But you do...live in sin, that is."

"Fresh!" said the girl.

"As this morning's milk, sweetheart," replied Splinters. "But that's an utter story."

They left, slamming the door hard.

***

In the club, the last customer staggered out the door. Polly, the head waitress, emptied the ashtrays.

"How was it tonight?" Willy asked.

"About the same as always," said Polly, "maybe a little better since there were more drunks than usual. I won't know till I ring up the tabs."

"Why? Do folks tip more when they're drunk?" asked Willy.

Polly laughed. "Are you kidding? No way. Once the jerks are good and drunk, I start overcharging them and adding drinks they never ordered to the tab. Then I pocket the difference."

"That don't sound very honest," said Willy.

"Hey, a girl's gotta make a living."

Willy walked behind the bar. A cold glass of ginger ale was just what he needed. He took one of the glasses and filled it full of ice.

"No, Willy, don't use that glass," said Karl the bartender.

"Why not?"

"It's not clean."

"What do you mean? It was down with rest of the clean glasses," said Willy.

Karl took the glass and emptied the ice in the sink. "The row to the left is my revenge glasses."

"Revenge glasses?" Willy questioned.

"Yeah, I keep a few glasses for customers who give me a hard time or are lousy tippers. Those glasses I spit in."

Willy cringed. His urge for a ginger ale left him. He decided to change the subject.

"Say, Karl, do you know where the boss is?"

"Probably in his office counting his money, the cheap bum."

"Thanks," said Willy as he started off.

Karl called out to him. "Why don't you step outside for a minute? Denny just bought a new car. The kid gets a big kick out of showing it off; he's real proud of it."

"I'll do that," Willy said, turning and walking out the front door.

Denny was the club's parking attendant. He was a handsome, young man with a winning smile.

Everyone liked Denny. Outside, Willy found the parking lot near empty except for the cars of the club workers. Denny was counting his night's tips.

"Hey, Denny, how did it go tonight?" Willy asked.

"No bad," Denny replied. "Not bad at all."

"Karl told me you got a new car."

"Yeah, that's it over there," Denny said, pointing at a sleek, red sports car parked close to the front of the club. "Ain't she a honey?" Denny said proudly.

"It sure is," Willy answered back. "Where did you get the money for a car like that? It must have set you back a pretty penny. I'm in the wrong business. Maybe I should give up showbiz and start parking cars?"

"I'll let you in on a little secret," Denny whispered, looking around to make sure there were no straggling customers still around. "People leave some expensive things in their cars. I've got their keys, see. While they're in the club, I'm looking under the seats, in their glove compartments, and in their trunks. It's usually weeks before they notice anything's missing."

"That doesn't sound right," Willy said.

"Don't be a sap. Everyone steals. My motto is 'do to others before they do it to you'; and they will, you know."

Willy shook his head and let out a sigh of disbelief and disappointment. Back in the club, he walked backstage to the owner's office. He knocked on the door.

A voice seeped through the door. "Who is it?"

"Mr. Lombardy, it's me, Willy."

"Come in, Willy."

He entered and found Mr. Lombardy's desk covered with dozens of empty liquor bottles. Willy recognized the labels; they were all top brands. Mr. Lombardy put a funnel in one of the empty bottles and filled it with the contents from a bottle of cheap, grocery-store liquor. He capped that bottle, put the funnel in the next bottle and repeated the process.

"Be with you in a minute, Willy. It's the time of the month when I have to restock the bar."

"Isn't that illegal?" Willy asked.

"Of course it's illegal. But who's gonna know? I put cheap booze in the bottles of expensive booze, plus ten percent water. People are stupid. They can't tell the good stuff from the cheap stuff. They see the label, and that's all their little brains and flavor buds need to know. Besides, all they want to do is get drunk anyways. The cheap stuff does just as good a job, and it puts a little more money in my pocket."

Mr. Lombardy capped the bottle and sat down at his desk.

"So, Willy, what can I do for you?"

"I hate to ask," said Willy, "but could I have an advance on my pay?"

"Payday is Friday, Willy."

"I know, sir; but I've got no money; and they locked us out of the hotel."

"Us?" asked Lombardy. "What's this 'Us' stuff? What do you have…a woman?"

"Mr. Lombardy, please."

"I'd like to help you, Willy; but I can't. If I give you an advance, then everyone will start asking for one." He thought for a moment. "I'll tell you what I'll do. You can spend the rest of the week in your dressing room."

Willy realized it was useless and decided to accept the offer. "Thank you, Mr. Lombardy," said Willy as he left the office.

He heard Mr. Lombardy call to him through the closed door. "Payday's on Friday. See ya then, Willy."

Walking back to his dressing room, he met the two showgirls.

"That was pretty clever the way you got your dummy to talk to us when you weren't there. But we don't appreciate the way you spoke to us. It was downright rude."

Immediately, Willy understood what happened. "Sorry, ladies; it will never happen again."

"See that it doesn't," said the other showgirl. They huffed and puffed as they walked away.

Back in the dressing room, Willy sat on the couch next to Splinters.

"Well, I couldn't get any money. But Mr. Lombardy says we can stay here in our dressing room."

"What a peach of a guy," said Splinters.

"Splinters," said Willy as he leaned across the couch and shut off the light, "please, watch what you say from now on. You've got to learn to bite your tongue."

"Willy, I don't have a tongue."

"You know what I mean. Don't try to be funny."

"That's the problem with our act, Willy; neither one of us is that funny."

***

The next night was the same. Willy and Splinters sat center stage under a white-hot spotlight. Willy was sweating bullets. Splinters would have been also if he were capable of sweating. The crowd was rough.

"Heard any new jokes that you'd like to tell these good people?" Willy asked.

The smile left Splinters' face. "Good? Good? It is written: 'There is no one good, not one. There is no one who understands; there is no one who seeks God. All have turned away; they have become worthless; there is no one who does good, not even one. Their throats are open graves; their tongues practice deceit; vipers' poison is on their lips. Their mouths are full of cursing and bitterness. Their feet are swift to shed blood. Ruin and misery mark their way, and the way of peace they do not know.' Good? Good? Not this roomful of dummies."

A worried look swept over Willy's face.

"Don't worry, Willy; no one's listening. They need to be, but they're not. Say, do you want to hear some imitations?"

Willy knew that when Splinters was on a spree, there was no stopping him, so he reluctantly gave an approving nod.

Splinters opened his mouth, and the roar of a police siren came out of his mouth. It was as loud and real-sounding as a siren. This caught the crowd's attention. Everyone went silent, stopped what they were doing, and looked up at the two figures on the stage. The siren stopped.

"There's a tape recorder inside the dummy," someone hollered.

"The only thing inside me, pal, is this guy's hand," Splinters announced. "Here, listen to this." He opened his mouth, and the sound of a foghorn came out. It shook the building. When he stopped, the crowd jumped to their feet and applauded. Mr. Lombardy came rushing out of his office. Karl stopped pouring drinks. Polly and the waitstaff stopped serving. Denny stood in the doorway, wondering what all the noise was about. All eyes were on Willy and Splinters.

"I can do impersonations, too," said Splinters. "Here, listen." His lips moved up and down. "Today I consider myself the luckiest man on the face of the earth." It was the Lou Gehrig speech, complete with the Yankee Stadium echo.

The crowd cheered wildly. "Do another one," someone shouted.

Splinter threw back his head. "Ask not what your country can do for you; ask what you can do for your country." Then, without a pause, "Mr. Gorbachev, tear down this wall."

"Hey, he sounds just like them guys," someone yelled over the cheers and howls.

"Would you like me to do some impersonations of some of the folks here tonight?" Splinters asked.

"Yeah!" roared the crowed in unison.

"Okay, here it goes," Splinters said. The room went silent, everyone wanting to hear every word. Out of Splinters' mouth came a flawless impersonation of Polly the waitress. "Once the jerks are good and drunk, I start overcharging them and adding drinks they never ordered to the tab. Then I pocket the difference."

There wasn't a sound from the audience; the room remained silent. All jaws dropped. Some of the regulars looked at Polly with disappointment and angry eyes. Splinters continued. This time it was the unmistakable voice of

Karl, the bartender. "I keep a few glasses for customers who give me a hard time or are lousy tippers. Those glasses I spit in."

You could hear a pin drop. Everyone stopped drinking.

Splinters continued. "People leave some expensive things in their cars. I've got their keys, see.

While they're in the club, I'm looking under the seats, in their glove compartments, and in their trunks. It's usually weeks before they notice anything's missing."

Everyone understood this to be an impression of the young man outside who had parked their car.

"And now for everyone's favorite," announced Splinters. "I put cheap booze in the bottles of expensive booze, plus ten percent water. People are stupid. They can't tell the good stuff from the cheap stuff. They see the label, and that's all their little brains and flavor buds need to know. Besides, all they want to do is get drunk anyways. The cheap stuff does just as good a job, and it puts a little more money in my pocket."

Heads turned, and all eyes darted at Mr. Lombardy standing at the edge of the stage. Quietly and orderly, everyone walked out of the club. The spotlight on Willy and Splinters went black.

***

At the corner bus stop, Willy sat on a bench under a beam of light coming from a streetlamp. He was waiting on the midnight bus out of town. There were two large suitcases at his feet. One held his belongings; the other held Splinters.

Splinters' muffled voice came seeping out of the suitcase. "You're not mad at me, are you, Willy?"

"I'm not talking to you," Willy said.

"Too late, you just did," replied Splinters.

"What gets into you?" pleaded Willy.

"I can't help it," said Splinters. "I just gotta say what needs to be said. You know what the Good Book says, 'The truth will set you free'."

"Yeah, free to look for another job," replied Willy.

"Willy, you can't remain silent when another person's soul hangs in the balance. But if you want me to, I'll never say another word again. We could go back to the way it was when you did all the talking."

Willy sighed. "No, you're right. I wouldn't know what to say, and you always say it best, even if it's hard sometimes."

"That's the spirit," said Splinters.

"Hush now," said Willy. "Here comes the bus."

THE END

35

UNHEARD VOICES

She stood in the wings, listening to her introduction. Her entourage was around her, making sure everything was perfect. There was electricity in the air.

"And now, the moment you've been waiting for, a woman who needs no introduction, the grand dame of the movement: Dr. Janet Cutter!"

When Cutter hit the stage, every one of the ten thousand stood up and cheered. She stood at the podium, waiting for a silence that did not come for three minutes. Finally, when everyone was seated and quiet, she moved in closer to the microphone.

"Thank you. As I approach the winter of my life, it is good to see so many young faces here today. Yes, I was there years ago at the beginning when the only choice a woman had was a backroom that wasn't sterile and a coat hanger wielded by unclean, unsafe, untrained hands. I can't begin to tally the numbers of lost or shattered lives.

"But I'm not bitter; nor should you be. You need to be gentle and patient with friends and family who oppose you. They base their opinions on myths, lies, and misinformation. It is your job, no…your duty…to educate them. Knowledge must be your weapon.

"Before the legalization of abortion, countless women died or were maimed. Marriages were doomed. Thousands of unwanted babies were born to a life of poverty, misery, and, in many cases, deformity.

"Our work is not only for ourselves, but for future generations. The course of society and the very earth is in our hands.

"Yes, I was there at the beginning. For years we fought. We voted; we petitioned; we marched; and yes, many of us, me included, were arrested. But it was worth it. In 1973 abortion became legal in this country, better late than never. Think of the misery that could have been prevented if the law were past just one year earlier."

Cutter stopped speaking, blinked, and squinted. As she looked out at the audience, she felt something was wrong; but she couldn't put her finger on it. She decided to ignore the feeling and continue.

"And I'm just talking about the difference one year would have made. What if the law were passed five years earlier? Think of what a better country we would be living in today."

She stopped again. This time, it was more than a feeling. Clearly, a third of the audience was missing. There were empty seats everywhere. It was full capacity when she came on stage. How could a third of the people disappear in the blink of an eye? She continued with her speech, hesitantly.

"Even better, what a better *world* it would be, if they passed the law at the beginning when we started the movement in the sixties?"

Cutter stopped speaking. There was no question in her mind now. Half of the audience was gone…disappeared. She felt faint. There was silence for a moment, and then people started to mumble. She backed away from the podium and walked to the wing of the stage. Her secretary and confidant, Linda Moray, rushed to her.

"Janet, are you all right?"

"Something's wrong. I don't feel well. I don't think I can continue. Give them my apologies. I'd like to go back to the hotel now."

"Of course," Linda said, taking hold of the old woman's arm and guiding her through the crowd and outside to the limo.

Cutter looked around. She only saw three of the five people in her entourage.

"Where are Cooper and Warwick?" Cutter asked.

"Where is who? I don't know any Cooper or Warwick," Linda replied. Fearing things might be worse than they seemed, Linda opened the door of the limo and guided Dr. Cutter into the backseat. She turned to the others, "Meet us at the hotel. I'm taking her straight there."

As Linda jumped into the back of the limo, she disappeared. The door slammed, and Cutter was alone.

"Linda! Linda, where did you go?" Cutter cried.

"Excuse me, ma'am?" asked the limo driver.

"Where's Linda," Cutter shouted, "the young woman I came with?"

"Sorry, ma'am, but I don't remember a Linda. You came by yourself. Would you like to go back to the hotel?"

"Yes, take me back to the hotel," Cutter muttered. She remained silent, trying to figure what was happening. Why were some people not only disappearing, but when they did it was as if they never existed? "As if they'd never been born," Cutter said out loud.

"How's that, ma'am?" the driver asked.

She spoke louder. "If a person is destined to be born, but you prevent them from being born, do you think that causes a gap in the universe?"

He smirked a little. "I wouldn't know about such things, ma'am."

In that very instant, he disappeared. Cutter tried to jump into the front seat and take hold of the steering wheel. But it was too late. The limo crashed into a streetlamp.

When Cutter came to, she was on a gurney in the back of an emergency vehicle. Checking her vital signs was a young man.

"How old are you?" Cutter asked.

"Don't speak," he said. "You need to keep your strength."

Cutter blinked and the young man was gone. A stethoscope lay on her chest.

At the hospital, they wheeled her in through the emergency entrance. Inside, they leaned her gurney against a wall. A nurse gave her the once-over and then walked over to another nurse. They spoke softly, but Cutter could hear what they said.

"That old woman doesn't look good. I think she's bleeding internally."

"I'm afraid she'll have to wait," said the second nurse. "We just don't have enough staff. Give her something for her pain. The least we can do is to make her comfortable."

Cutter felt her body grow limp. The world was growing dark. She suspected she was dying. Then she blacked out.

***

When she came to, she was standing at the wings of the stage in the same spot she had stood only a few hours before. Linda was at her side.

"And now, the moment you've been waiting for, a woman who needs no introduction, the grand dame of the movement: Dr. Janet Cutter!"

Cutter walked up to the podium. For the second time that day, she waited for the roar of the crowd to die down. When everyone was seated and all was quiet, she leaned into the microphone.

"Yes, I was there from the beginning!" Cutter announced to cheers and whistles. "We fought long and hard for what we thought was right!" There were more cheers. "And in all those years, I found it curious that everyone who worked or voted or marched or petitioned for abortion had one thing in common: they were all living. They were all alive."

The crowd went silent; in their confusion they mumbled among themselves. Cutter continued. "They were the ones who'd made it under the wire. They were alive. They wanted what they wanted; and if it meant someone else not ever getting to be alive, well, that was just fine by them. They never thought, 'Gee, what if abortion was legal when I was born? Maybe I wouldn't be here? But they didn't care because they were already alive. They never considered that if a person is taken out of the equation, perhaps the answer to that equation will never be answered. What if the person you stopped from being born could have made a difference in this stinking world? Maybe it would leave a hole in the universe that will never be filled. We raised our voices for what we wanted; but there were millions of tiny voices that will never be heard, who will never get what they want."

The crowd became angry. They booed and hissed and threw things up on the stage.

Cutter spoke louder and directly into the microphone. "I don't know when life begins, no more than anyone else here; but I'm going to try to find out. But I tell you, until I do know when life begins, as a *human being*, I will always stand on the side of life because that is the moral thing to do!"

She walked off stage. Backstage, everyone moved aside to let her walk by. Some of them refused to look at her; some cursed her as she went by. Outside, in front of the limo, no one was there to open the door for her. None of the people backstage, not even her entourage had followed her. But strangely enough, she did not feel alone. She sat down in the back of the limo.

"Where to, ma'am?" asked the driver.

"Just drive," said Janet. "I'll know when we get there."

THE END

36

A DONKEY'S TALE

It was a good life. The barn was large, warm; and all the stalls were clean. The master made sure they always had hay, feed, and fresh water. They were a happy family, most of the time.

There were the two horses: Buster – so named because he could bust down a stall with a single kick; and his wife, Whinny Neigh…because that's what she did throughout the day. There was Brownie the cow, because she was solid brown from nose to tail and from horn to huff. The two goats: Billy – because that's what he was, and Nanny – because that's what she was. Mother Hen – could lay more eggs in a single day and hatch them in a week, faster than any other chicken in Jerusalem; and her dashing husband, First Up, who rose before all the others every morning and began crowing to wake the entire neighborhood. Lastly, there was Jenny the donkey and her newborn foal, Young Colt.

Mother Hen sat on a pile of hay in the middle of the barn, keeping six newly laid eggs under her. "Oh, I do hope the master doesn't take any of my eggs for his breakfast. I'd like to see all of them hatch," she said.

"They knew what they were doing when they named you Mother Hen. That's all you ever think about," First Up said as he pecked at seeds in the dust.

"Now, dear, don't take this wrong," Whinny Neigh said to Mother Hen. "We were all talking and wondering why you always built your nest in the middle of the barn."

"Why, what does it matter?" Mother Hen asked.

"Because it makes it hard for the rest of us to move about," Brownie complained as she kicked her milk pail in frustration.

"But the center is where the most light shines," Mother Hen huffed.

"You don't understand," Buster said. "You're so small, and I am so large. Sometimes I can hardly move for fear of crushing your eggs."

"But it's the warmest spot in the barn," Mother Hen insisted.

"No, it isn't," Jenny said. "The far wall…the master lives on the other side of it. That's where his fireplace is. It's always warm, especially when his wife is cooking and at night."

"Well, I don't know," Mother Hen said, jumping from her nest, rushing to the far wall, and placing her wing on it. "It does feel rather warm."

Billy Goat walked over to Mother Hen's nest and examined the eggs. "I've never eaten an egg before," he said. "I bet they taste real good."

"Get away from my eggs!" Mother Hen shouted, running toward him, shooing him away. She hopped back on her nest.

"Billy was only fooling," Nanny Goat said. "My husband would never eat your eggs. Would you, dear?"

"I wouldn't? Oh, no, of course not," Billy said.

Young Colt's timid voice came from the shadows, behind his mother. "It doesn't bother me if Mother Hen puts her nest in the center of the barn."

"And who asked your opinion?" First Up clucked.

"Let Young Colt speak," Buster said.

"Young Colt…what kind of name is Young Colt? That's not a proper name," First Up said.

"Leave him be," Brownie said. "We've all come to our names for what we've done in our lives. He's still young. Give him time. He'll earn a proper name."

Jenny came to the defense of her son. "One day he will do something great and he will have a great name."

"Really?" said First Up. "Like what? Hay Eater? Daydreamer?"

"Hush up, all of you. Someone's coming," Nanny whispered. All the animals fell silent.

The barn door opened, and two men walked in. They went straight to Jenny and Young Colt.

"Here they are," said one of the men, taking hold of Jenny's reins.

Suddenly, the master of the house rushed in, holding a pitchfork. "What are you two doing?" he shouted, pointing the pitchfork at the two men. "This is my barn and these are my animals."

"This is not what you think," one of the men pleaded.

The other man stood directly in front of the pitchfork, the prongs pointing at his chest. "The Lord has need of them. They will be returned to you."

As if in a trance, the man put his pitchfork down and let them pass by him and guide Jenny and Young Colt. The master left also.

Once alone, the animals talked among themselves.

"The Lord has need of them.' What does that mean?" Billy said.

"And who is this 'Lord' person?" Nanny asked.

"You don't think they'll eat them?" Whinny Neigh wondered aloud.

"Of course not," Buster said. "People don't eat donkeys. They eat chickens and cows and goats."

"Not as long as they lay eggs," Mother Hen said.

"Not as long as they give milk," Brownie said.

"Quiet! Listen, do you hear that?" Nanny said.

They all listened. They heard the sound of many people shouting in the streets.

"You don't think that has anything to do with Jenny and Young Colt?" Whinny Neigh asked.

"They've seen donkeys before," Brownie said. "This is something else."

The roar of the crowd passing the barn grew louder. Buster went and looked out through a crack in the door. "There are hundreds of humans in the streets. They're singing and dancing and carrying palm leaves. Wait, I see Jenny. The crowd is making way for Jenny. And there's Young Colt. There's a man riding him."

"Why would anyone ride Young Colt when they could ride Jenny? It doesn't make any sense," First Up said.

"Humans have never made sense to me," Mother Hen proclaimed.

"What's happening now?" Whinny Neigh asked Buster.

"They're moving on, and the crowd is following them. They're going…going… gone. I can't see anyone now."

It was true. The sound of the crowd faded slowly till all they heard was silence. Buster moved away from the door and back near Whinny Neigh. They waited quietly, not knowing what to say. They waited a long time, when the door suddenly opened; and the two men from before came in with Jenny and Young Colt.

"Thank you, little donkey," said one of the men as he petted Young Colt on the head. They turned and left, closing the barn door behind them.

When they had gone, all the animals rushed to Jenny.

"Are you all right? What happened? What was that about?" each of them asked in turn.

"It was a parade to honor the man with many names," Jenny said.

"Many names? How can someone have many names?" First Up said, shaking his head. "You get named for what you do, and that's it."

"Maybe this man does many different things?" Nanny said.

"What names did they call him?" Buster asked.

Jenny continued. "Mostly they call him 'Hosanna,' but some called him 'Lord,' and some called him 'Master'. While others called him God. Whatever that means?"

"And that's how I got my name," Young Colt said.

"You have a name, now?" First Up asked.

"Yes, the people shouted my new name."

"What is it?" Buster asked.

"Highest."

"Highest? I don't understand," First Up said.

"It was the crowd who gave him the name," Jenny said. "The man who rode on him was named 'God'. And they all shouted, 'Glory to God on the Highest'." Jenny smiled at her son and then spoke with pride. "From this day on, my son will be known as 'Highest'."

All the animals bowed and spoke as one. "Welcome home, Highest."

THE END

Michael Edwin Q. is available for book interviews and personal appearances. For more information contact:

Michael Edwin Q.
C/O Advantage Books
P.O. Box 160847
Altamonte Springs, FL 32716
michaeledwinq.com

To purchase additional copies of this book visit our bookstore website at: www.advbookstore.com

Longwood, Florida, USA
"we bring dreams to life"™
www.advbookstore.com